WILD NIGHT

WILDER IRISH, BOOK 10

MARI CARR

This story is dedicated to the "original" Kelli Collins, my editor for the past sixteen years. She's walked every mile in the Wild/Wilder Irish series with me and I couldn't live a day without her.

With Wild Night, she is now a legitimate member of the family!

WILD NIGHT

Confirmed bachelor Colm is living the good life with a thriving law practice and all the freedom the playboy has come to enjoy. Until a city-wide blackout and the greatest sex he's ever had has him reconsidering his single status. Unfortunately, he doesn't realize the woman of his dreams is actually his lifelong frenemy, Kelli.

After a few too many drinks at a Halloween party, Kelli spends the night in the arms of a man who rocks her world. However, when she learns her mystery Mr. Right is Mr. Hell No, Colm Collins, she's ready to run for the hills.

But Colm refuses to accept just one wild night with her. He wants them all and the sexy man plays dirty.

C olm Collins walked into the pub, climbed onto the stool next to Patrick, dropped his bookbag on the floor, and slouched back in the seat, managing to look completely bored in three seconds.

"How was school, lad?" Patrick asked.

While his young grandson had a genial disposition, he didn't wear his emotions on his sleeve like his twin brother, Padraig, who was always quick with a laugh and rarely without a smile. Rather, Colm was more thoughtful, introspective, and, well, mischievous.

Colm shrugged. "It was alright."

Padraig, who'd come in right behind him, tossed his bookbag to the floor next to his brother's. Typically, the boys got off the bus after school at home, but their mother, Lane, a nurse at Johns Hopkins, was working second shift, as was Patrick's son, Tris—the boys' father—who was currently manning the bar here at the pub.

The boys, at fifteen, were certainly old enough to stay

home alone, but Colm had been caught sneaking his new girlfriend—the boy seemed to have a new love every other minute—into his bedroom two nights earlier. As such, Lane and Tris had grounded him and decided he would not be staying at the house alone until they could trust him again.

Patrick feared recovering that trust might not be a quick process. A teenage boy's hormones were a powerful thing.

Tris returned from the kitchen with clean glasses, nodding at the boys when he saw them. "You guys have homework?"

From his gruff tone, it was apparent Tris was still unhappy about Colm's behavior and determined to make this punishment memorable.

"Yeah, some. It won't take me too long though," Padraig said. "Want me to help you put the glasses away?" Padraig had obviously decided to share in the punishment with his brother, rather than go home alone. Which wasn't surprising. Padraig loved being in the pub, helping his father with various tasks.

Tris grinned. "Sure. Colm, why don't you grab that booth over there—where I can keep an eye on you—and start your homework. We're eating dinner here, and I've got one of the part-time bartenders coming in to close up. Might as well settle in. You're going to be here for a while."

Colm sighed and rolled his eyes, but—wisely—held his tongue as he stood up to do as he was told.

Patrick fought to hide his grin. As the father of four rowdy, always-pushing-curfews-and-rules boys, he knew Tris was only just at the beginning of this battle with his intelligent, girl-crazy son.

"Mind if I join you for a few minutes, Colm?" Patrick asked, rising as well.

His clever grandson considered the question for a moment, obviously concerned he was about to get another lecture for his behavior. Patrick gave him a quick, covert wink to assure him he was safe.

Colm grinned. "Sure. That's cool, Pop Pop."

Colm retrieved his backpack and the two of them crossed the pub, claiming a booth in the corner. It was midafternoon, so the pub would be quiet until the happy hour crowd started to roll in.

"Are you going to yell at me too?" Colm asked once they were seated.

"I hadn't planned to. I suspect your parents said all that needed to be said."

Colm lifted one shoulder casually. "I guess so."

"Am I to assume the young lady in question was the one you were telling me about a couple of weeks ago? I believe her name was Jessica."

Colm shook his head. "No. Me and Jess are history. I'm going out with Zoey now."

"My, my. I might need to start a list. I'm struggling to keep the names of your lady loves straight."

Colm laughed. "You don't need to worry about learning names yet. I'm just having some fun. Paddy's the one who wants a girlfriend, not me."

"I see. Padraig doesn't have a girlfriend, though, right?"

Colm shook his head. "Nope. Not right now anyway. Paddy's too picky. I'm not criticizing, Pop Pop, but I think you've been a bad influence on him."

Patrick tilted his head curiously. "In what way?"

"He's always looking for *the one*. Like last year. He starts dating Stephanie Bell, swears she's the girl for him, then gets his heart broken. Like we couldn't all see that coming. All the dude wants to do is fall in love like you and Grandma Sunday."

"I see." And this was why Patrick asked to join Colm at this booth. His precocious fifteen-year-old grandson was wise beyond his years, sarcastic, intelligent, and funny. "And you don't have those same aspirations?"

"Heck no. I'm gonna be young while I'm young. Not planning to settle down until I'm forty, at least. Paddy will probably elope three seconds after high school. Not that that's so surprising."

"Because of his tendency to fall in love too fast?"

"No. Because he doesn't have my way with the ladies. That's why he falls so fast whenever a girl pays attention to him. Always been that way. Did you know he actually paid for his first kiss?"

"Paid for it?"

"Yeah. Kelli charged him a quarter when we were in fifth grade."

Patrick chuckled. Kelli Peterson had been Padraig's best friend since elementary school, the girl a familiar face at Tris and Lane's home and even here at the pub. "Is that right?"

"Yeah. She charged a couple other guys too."

"Quite the enterprising young lady. Am I to assume you didn't pay for the same?"

"Pop Pop," Colm said with a cocky grin. "First of all, it was Kelli. Gross."

Patrick had always found it interesting how very different Colm was from his brother. While Kelli and

Padraig were truly the best of friends, Colm seemed to view the same girl with genuine disdain. He'd always wondered if those feelings were based on personality differences or if Colm felt jealousy toward Kelli, unhappy about sharing his twin brother.

"And secondly," Colm continued. "The ladies should be paying me to kiss *them*."

Patrick hid his mouth behind his hand. It wouldn't help Tris and Lane's cause if he laughed, though he was thoroughly amused by Colm's cockiness. The boy wasn't lacking when it came to confidence. "So no long-term girlfriends for you?"

"Nope. I'm free as a bird and plan to stay that way." Colm leaned back, slouching slightly in the booth, assuming a look that couldn't be called anything other than pure teenage male confidence. If Colm was walking right now, he'd be swaggering. Patrick was familiar with the look because he'd seen the exact same thing in Colm's father, Tris, when he was young.

Glancing toward the bar, Patrick wondered if Tris realized how close this apple had fallen to the tree. Lane had suggested more than a few times that Colm and Tris butted heads as often as they did because they were birds of a feather.

"Free as a bird, eh?" Patrick repeated. "Well, then your name certainly fits you."

Colm rolled his eyes. "Yeah, yeah. I'm a freaking dove. You know how lame that is, right?"

Patrick had gotten into the habit of telling his young grandchildren the meanings of their names, sharing stories of past namesakes who'd gone on to do incredible things. Colm had been incredibly unimpressed by the meaning of his name, and even less enthusiastic by the story of the name-sake, St. Columba, whose monks created *The Book of Kells*.

"The dove represents peace, Colm. That's a wonderful thing."

Colm, who'd been in the process of pulling a notebook out of his backpack, paused. "Lochlan gets Viking. Finn gets warrior, and I get peace. Lame," he repeated.

Patrick chuckled, aware that in this instance, he didn't have a leg to stand on. "Your mother found the name in a baby book. Be grateful she went for Colm rather than her first choice."

Colm frowned. "What was her first choice?"

"Peter. She thought Padraig and Peter sounded cute together. Your father put his foot down."

Colm appeared surprised. "I never knew that. What does Peter mean?"

"Stone."

"I'll take the dove."

Patrick nodded. "Wise choice." They fell silent for a few minutes as Colm opened his notebook, then reached back into his backpack for a textbook. While Patrick knew Padraig didn't have much homework, he was certain the same wasn't true for Colm, who was taking all honors classes, unlike his twin, who viewed high school as something he simply had to tolerate for four years.

"What are you working on?"

Colm wrinkled his nose. "*Romeo and Juliet*. Dumbest play in history."

"You're starting to hurt my soul, lad. That's a very romantic story."

"Romantic? Um. Did you read all the way to the end? Spoiler alert, Pop Pop. They both die."

Patrick grinned. "Maybe so, but I've always liked the true love aspect."

Colm was too polite to roll his eyes at Patrick, though his expression said that was exactly what he wanted to do. "They fell in love in a hot minute. That's not real life."

"Oh, but you're wrong, my boy. That's exactly how it happened for me and Sunday. She was singing at the bar, and I knew—all the way to my bones—that she was the one for me."

Colm studied his face intently, then shook his head slowly. "I don't think that's when you fell in love. It doesn't work that way."

Patrick smiled and considered that. Whenever he told the story of the night he first met Sunday, he always proclaimed it was love at first sight. But when he really thought about it, it was an entire series of moments that came to mind, all of them building on each other.

"Well now. Perhaps you might be right about that."

"Really?"

"Yes. Now that I think about it, I fell for her more slowly than I first thought. There was an instant attraction, of course, but the love grew as we got to know each other better, as we shared our hopes and dreams for the future and realized we were both walking in the same direction. You know, love has a way of sneaking up on a person, showing up at the most unexpected times. One look, one word, one random moment in time and then...it's just...click. The light flips on and even the darkest of hearts is filled with bright, radiant light."

"Just click?" Colm didn't seem convinced, but he was definitely listening.

And interested.

"Just click. And when it happens, it's magic."

Colm was quiet for a moment, and then his all-too-familiar lopsided grin emerged. "This is exactly what I'm talking about, Pop Pop. This is where Paddy gets all his ideas about love."

Patrick shrugged. "Guilty as charged, I suppose."

"Bad influence," Colm muttered, but Patrick saw the slightest flicker of something in his grandson's face, and he recognized it instantly.

Colm wanted the click.

CHAPTER ONE

Colm tossed back the rest of his Guinness, then glanced down toward the end of the bar at Pat's Pub. It was only Wednesday and he'd already had a bear of a week. As a lawyer who specialized in family law, he'd seen more than his fair share of contentious divorces, bitter custody battles, and tragic cases of domestic abuse. This week? He'd dealt with all three. Nasty shit. And it felt like it was ripping out chunks of his soul.

Typically, he could keep emotions out of it, could focus on the task at hand. If it had just been one case, he could have held it together. But he was dealing with three. The three worst cases of his career. All at the same time.

He caught Padraig's eye and pointed to his empty mug. His twin narrowed his eyes briefly, but Padraig knew him well enough that he didn't question him. Instead, he just picked up the empty mug, pulled the tap, refilled his glass, and then set it back down in front of him.

"Wanna talk about it?" Padraig asked.

Colm shook his head. "Nope. Just want to forget about it."

"Yeah, the fact you're on your third beer in less than an hour...on a weeknight...sort of clued me in. You sure you—"

"I'm sure," Colm interjected.

"Okay. Well, I'm here if you change your mind."

Colm managed a weak smile and a nod. He knew that, knew his brother would always listen to his troubles, would have his back in a fight, would give him shit whenever he did something stupid. They were brothers and that was what they did. Add in the whole twin-bond factor, and it was safe to say no one on the planet got him like Padraig.

He took another sip of his Guinness, leaning back in the stool, savoring the quiet white noise of the pub. This place, this very stool at the bar, was probably one of his happiest places on the planet. So as soon as he'd dragged his sorry ass in from work, he'd plopped down with no more thought than he was home and beer was close.

He loosened his necktie and unbuttoned the top button of his shirt, releasing a long sigh.

He could have walked right by the bar and headed upstairs to the apartment he shared with some of his cousins. After all, it was empty right now. Darcy had gotten a new job recently and had been putting in long hours, excited to prove herself as a graphic artist, while his other roomies, Oliver and Gavin, were working late at a construction site with Uncle Killian and Uncle Justin.

Colm would have had the entire apartment to himself, something that was rare, given the number of family members who treated the place—the Collins Dorm—as home base for...well...practically everything. Pretty much every Collins celebration took place either here in the pub or upstairs. From graduation parties to bridal showers, his huge, crazy, fun family always managed to find something to celebrate, and damn if they didn't do it in style.

Just this morning, Darcy was buzzing around the apartment, her excitement almost tangible as she pointed out that with their annual Halloween party happening this weekend, they were kicking off the official "Collins social season." After the Halloween party—which Sunnie and Darcy had been planning for ages—it was one festivity after another as they hosted Friendsgiving, Thanksgiving dinner, a Christmas party, and then rang in the New Year in serious style.

Colm was exhausted just thinking about it. Which was unusual for him. He always looked forward to family events, but this year...this year it felt like hard work.

Shit. The job really was getting to him.

He rubbed his eyes, then kept them closed, breathing in and out slowly. He'd almost found peace when there was a loud scratching sound of the stool next to him, sliding across the floor.

"Fucking fuck of a fucked-up day."

Colm sighed. He should have gone upstairs.

He didn't bother to open his eyes to acknowledge the new arrival. "Hey, Kell."

"What the fuck is wrong with you?"

He glanced over and saw her looking at him curiously.

"Were you asleep?" she asked.

He shook his head. "No. I was relaxing. And it was working. Until you showed up."

Kelli rolled her eyes, completely unrepentant about disturbing him. Not that he should be surprised. They knew each other far too well for her to ever genuinely take offense over anything he said. Same went for him.

Kelli had been Padraig's best friend since kindergarten. Leave it to his twin brother to pick a girl as his best friend. And not just a girl but Padraig's polar opposite. Padraig was an easy-going, quiet, gentle soul.

Kelli, on the other hand, was brash, loud, opinionated. She and Colm had butted heads for as many years as she and Padraig had been friends. Probably because, as Colm's mother liked to point out whenever he bitched about her, she and Colm were too much alike. Which Mom insisted was probably the reason why Padraig adored Kelli so. As if that was supposed to make him like her better.

"Hey, Paddy," Kelli called out when Padraig returned from the stockroom with a new bag of peanuts. "I need a glass of cab sav. A *big* glass."

"The nine-ounce pour?" Padraig teased.

"You stop at nine ounces and I'm going to kick your ass. Actually, save the glass. I'll just drink straight from the bottle."

Padraig laughed as he placed the wineglass in front of her, pouring red wine all the way to the rim.

Kelli lifted it gingerly, careful not to spill a single drop as she took a big sip, then sighed dramatically. "God, Paddy. You're the greatest man I've ever known."

Padraig rolled his eyes, then put the bottle of wine in

front of her. "Just in case I'm not here the second you drain that first glass."

"Marry me," she said, the joke a standard. Kelli had asked Padraig to marry her no less than seventeen million times over the years.

And Padraig always gave her the same response. "You're too much woman for me, Kell. It just wouldn't work."

"Speaking of marriage...where's Emmy?" Kelli asked, wiggling her eyebrows playfully at Padraig.

Only Kelli could get away with such a segue.

Over the course of the past year or so, Emmy Martin had become a regular at Pat's Pub, the quiet romance author achieving what only one other patron in the history of the business had managed. Her own saved spot at the bar. Padraig had placed a permanent reserved sign at the end of the counter for her since it was the place Emmy set up camp almost daily as she wrote her books.

The only other person with a saved stool was Pop Pop, though his was front and center, as the fun-loving man needed to be right in the thick of "the action" at the pub. Colm had figured out a long time ago that "action" meant Pop Pop had the seat with the best view of the big screen TV that hung behind the bar to watch whatever sport was in season, and a prime location for hearing any and all of the gossip shared.

Padraig pretended to be annoyed by the question. "Ha ha, Kell. Emmy is not here tonight."

Kelli had been trying to convince Padraig to ask Emmy out for months, but his twin wasn't budging.

Padraig had been married once to Mia, the love of his life. She had been everything to him. So even now, two years after her death, his brother was still struggling to put the pieces of his life back together.

Lately, Colm and Kelli had found one thing they actually agreed on, and that was that Padraig needed to move on with his life. He'd been hiding behind the counter of this pub for far too long.

Plus, as more time passed, it was pretty obvious Emmy had the hots for Padraig. And while he was resistant to romance, he and Emmy had formed a pretty solid friendship.

"Where is she?" Kelli pressed. "Emmy's always here. She's the reason I stopped by. I wanted to talk to her."

"She has a nasty head cold. I'm running some of Aunt Riley's chicken noodle soup over to her after my shift ends." Padraig looked at his watch. "Which is in about ten minutes."

"Taking her soup, huh?" Kelli asked. The woman was relentless when it came to Padraig and Emmy.

"As friends, Kell. I always bring you chicken noodle soup when you're sick too," Padraig pointed out.

"Yeah. Shit. You do. Come here. Lean closer."

Padraig sighed heavily, even as he did as she asked, perfectly aware of why Kelli had made the request.

She lifted her hand and stroked the side of his face. "I just can't get used to you without the beard."

Colm and Padraig had sported beards since the year they'd turned nineteen, placing a bet on who could grow one the fastest. Colm had won, something he still gave Padraig shit about, but even after the contest ended, neither of them shaved.

Then, out of the blue last week, Padraig had shown up at

the pub clean-shaven, simply telling everyone who asked why that he'd just needed a change.

Colm wondered if it wasn't something more, but no amount of questioning on his part—and he was a lawyer who knew how to get the goods from a witness—had produced a different response.

"How many times are you going to touch my face?" Padraig asked, though he didn't sound as annoyed as he pretended.

"It's just so strange."

"Good strange or bad strange?" Padraig asked.

Kelli considered that. "Good strange. Truth is...you look super hot like this."

"Please," Colm said, jumping into the conversation. "He has a baby face. You won't catch me shaving *my* beard off. Don't want to look like some wet-behind-the-ears teenage boy."

"You're just jealous because you couldn't pull off the look," Kelli said, jumping in, as always, to defend Padraig. It was another standard operating procedure. Kelli always—as in one hundred percent of the time—took Padraig's side in any argument with Colm, no matter what.

"That makes no sense," Colm said. "We're twins, Kelli. Identical. Twins."

"You know, I always forget that," she joked. "It probably has something to do with the shape of your mouth. The way it's always open and producing that annoying sound. Distracts me from all your other features."

Colm grinned and doubled-down. He'd had the day from hell, and the idea of blowing off some of that steam by engaging in a battle of put-downs with Kelli sounded pretty good to him. "The only annoying sound I hear right now is—"

"Oh, look at that," Padraig said, glancing at his phone. "My shift just ended."

While Colm and Kelli loved to trash talk, it drove Padraig up the wall. His brother really was too freaking nice sometimes.

Colm watched as Padraig's replacement, one of the new part-time bartenders, stepped through the hinged opening. His brother filled the new guy in on who was drinking what, and then said goodbye to them, heading back to the kitchen, no doubt to grab the soup for Emmy.

He and Kelli both took another sip of their drinks, neither of them bothering to pick up their previous conversation, and as the silence stretched, it occurred to Colm that the two of them were rarely alone together.

Kelli took another sip and, for the first time since she'd sat down, he noticed the dark circles under her eyes. She also hadn't changed out of her work attire before coming here, and he was amused by her orange sweater that featured a glittery black cat in bunny ears. She had a wide array of ridiculous clothing like that. He knew none of it fit her tastes, and that she wore it just because her kindergartners loved it.

She was taller than most women he knew, just an inch or so shy of six feet tall. Sometimes he wondered if that was why she'd continued to hang out with Padraig throughout school. He and his twin, at six foot four, were in the minority when it came to guys taller than her.

Her dark auburn hair had gotten longer in the last year. All through high school and their twenties, she'd kept it shorter, the thick, wavy mass barely touching her shoulders.

He wasn't sure what had prompted her to grow it out, but he had to admit—begrudgingly—it was very pretty on her. He liked long hair on women, gave him something to hold on to when he was...

Fuck.

He turned away from Kelli, unwilling to finish that thought.

For a hot minute, he'd had an image of taking her from behind, his fist gripping that long hair.

Jesus. Maybe he should lay off the Guinness.

Kelli sighed, capturing his attention again.

Oh, to fuck with it. She didn't annoy him so much that he couldn't admit she was actually very attractive. She had one of those unforgettable faces with high cheekbones, porcelain skin, full, red lips, and an ever-present twinkle in her eye that some might mistake for humor, but he recognized as mischief.

When she'd first gotten boobs in sixth grade—*big* boobs, the kind that captured a young boy's attention—Colm had fancied himself interested in her...for about three seconds.

Unfortunately, that was the same year his dad had thought he and Padraig should sport crewcuts, for some insane reason. His interest in Kelli ended the second she'd dubbed him "Chrome Dome Colm," the nickname sticking for the better part of the school year, before he'd put his foot down with his dad that summer and insisted on growing his hair out again.

After that, his crush on her had ended, and their rivalry had elevated from hair pulling and rude nicknames—she'd been Smelly Kelli most of first grade, thanks to him—to eye rolling, smirks, and practical jokes.

"So you had a bad day too?" he said.

She nodded once, then shrugged. "Lately, it's felt like one long string of bad days. But yeah, today was especially shitty."

When it became obvious she wasn't going to go into any details, he prodded. "What happened today?"

She glanced at him suspiciously, and he understood why. The two of them weren't small-talk friends. Actually, Kelli liked to refer to him as her best frenemy, something he hadn't bothered to deny since the term fit. If they were talking, they were bickering.

"My cat got sick in the middle of my new rug first thing this morning. I didn't see it, so I stepped in it, barefoot, and slipped. I hit the edge of the coffee table, so I now have a bruise on my hip the size of Kansas. Then I was running late to work, rushing around my place like a lunatic, looking for my goddamn keys, and I spilled coffee all over my outfit."

"That sweater wasn't your first choice?" Colm didn't bother to hide his grin.

Kelli didn't take him to task for it. Instead, she gave him a weary smile back. "All of that happened before eight a.m. Work wasn't much better. My hip hurt like a bitch. Believe me. Five-year-olds have sonar when it comes to sore spots. I swear every single one of the little rascals managed to bump into that exact spot today. Then one of my kids shit his pants —the smell was ungodly. After school, I had to sit through an eternal faculty meeting where we learned about a new round of budget cuts that basically ensure I'm going to continue to spend half my paycheck on supplies for my classroom."

"Damn."

"Yeah," she said, lifting her wineglass and draining it.

Colm reached over and poured her a new glass from the bottle Padraig had left in front of her.

"Thanks. So...that's why I'm willing to face tomorrow with a hangover. What number Guinness are you on?"

Colm drained his beer. "That was three." He lifted a finger and the part-time bartender came over and refilled it.

"Damn. Four beers," she murmured. "Wanna talk about it?"

Padraig had asked the same question, and he'd turned his brother down. For some reason, maybe given the fact she was in the same funk and the beer was starting to work its way through him, he didn't mind sharing with her.

"I'm working on a few rough cases. The worst of which is a contentious divorce with a custody battle that's going to guarantee the kids are in therapy for the rest of their lives."

Kelli frowned. "Young kids?"

For her tough exterior, Kelli was pure marshmallow inside when it came to children.

"Four and six."

"Fuck. Some people really shouldn't be allowed to have children. All they do is fuck them up."

"Yeah. Tell me about it. I'm also representing a woman in the middle of a domestic violence case, and I'm pretty sure she's going to drop the charges and go back with the man who put her in the hospital not once, not twice, but four times."

Kelli sighed. "Jesus. I don't know how you do that job."

Colm gave her a crooked grin. "Hey, at least I don't have to clean up shitty underwear."

Kelli tapped her wineglass against Colm's mug. "Good point. So...are we going to be the voice of reason for each other at the end of these drinks, or are we going to take this to the next level?"

The question was pure Kelli. He knew if he paid his tab and said good night, she'd follow suit. They'd both head home, pass out, and while they'd have headaches in the morning, they wouldn't be too much the worse for wear.

But if he ordered another beer, she'd finish the bottle of wine—and maybe even order another—and they'd both pay dearly at work tomorrow.

For Colm, there was only one answer. "Next level."

She grinned and took another sip. "Game on."

They continued to bitch about their days until her bottle of wine was drained and he'd finished beers number five and six. After that, they moved on to tequila, though at least they'd been somewhat intelligent and ordered food as well. They complained about their jobs until the bartender yelled out "last call."

"What time is it?" she asked.

Colm glanced at his phone. "Almost midnight."

"Damn. Made a critical error. Came to the wrong Collins twin for moral support. Paddy would have switched me to coffee after glass number two and poured me into a cab."

Colm shrugged unapologetically. "Hey, you gave me a choice."

"Yeah, I did." She glanced toward the door. "I guess I should..."

"Did you drive here?"

She nodded. "Really only intended to have one glass of wine while I chewed Paddy's ear off."

"Come upstairs. You can sleep in Finn's room. Sheets are

clean. Set your alarm early enough that you can go home, shower, and suffer through a hungover Thursday."

Kelli stood up. "That sounds perfect. I don't feel like being alone tonight."

Colm felt the exact same way.

CHAPTER TWO

K elli was no stranger to sleepovers at the Collins Dorm—the name Aunt Riley had given the apartment above the pub. She, like so many of the Collins friends, had spent countless nights there, either after too many drinks or simply because it was late and they were tired. Now that so many of Colm's cousins—and his brother—had moved out, there was plenty of room.

The two of them settled their tabs, then trudged upstairs. Kelli started to turn toward the staircase that led to the third floor, where Colm's room and what had been his cousin Finn's room, until he'd moved out, were located.

Colm stopped her. "I'm not tired."

She laughed. "Yeah. Me either. God. We're going to be totally fucked tomorrow."

She was right, but he was keyed up, wired. It was strange, given how completely wiped out he'd been after work. He walked over to the couch and dropped down heavily. "Guess Darcy and the guys have already turned in for the night."

"Looks like." Oliver, Darcy, and Gavin had all stopped by to chat for a few minutes as they'd returned home from work before heading upstairs.

Kelli followed him, claiming the other side of the couch. "Do you regret your chosen career?"

It made sense that Kelli had gotten that impression after listening to his work horror stories the past few hours. "Not a bit."

"I'm glad. Paddy told me once he worried about you, about how hard you work, but that he understood the reason why. That it was because of your mom."

"You know our mom was in foster care when she was a kid."

Kelli nodded. "I do."

Colm's mother, Lane, had grown up in the system, and while she'd shared bits and pieces of her childhood, it was evident her upbringing had been rough. When Colm decided to study law, specializing in family law felt like a no-brainer because he wanted to do as much as he possibly could to make sure other kids didn't suffer the same fate as his mother.

"So it makes sense that you'd want to help kids who might find themselves in that same position," Kelli continued. "Much as it pains me to say it, I've always admired you for that."

"Damn, Kell," he joked. "I bet that hurt."

"So fucking much," she muttered.

"You still happy wiping shitty asses and finger painting every day?"

"I'm teaching children how to read and write and learn to live in society as decent human beings. And yes, I'm happy with my decision." There was no heat behind her words as she set him straight.

"It's an admirable profession."

She looked at Colm, waiting for the punch line. He didn't have one. He knew for a fact she had a hard job, and he also knew she was damn good at it. God knew he couldn't spend seven hours a day in a room with twenty-eight five-year-olds for the shitty pay she got.

"Thanks," she said at last.

It occurred to Colm that this was the longest the two of them had ever been alone together, and civil. Whenever Kelli came around, it was to see Padraig or his cousins, Yvonne, Darcy, or Sunnie. Any conversations between the two of them were had while surrounded by his family, and they consisted solely of playful jabs.

"You still seeing Brooke?" she asked.

"Yup."

She grinned. "Doesn't bother you that she was totally into Paddy first? Sort of makes you the backup twin, doesn't it? Sloppy seconds?"

"Gross." Colm knew she was teasing him, but he bit anyway. "She and Paddy only went out on a couple of dates. They weren't in a relationship and they didn't engage in more than one good-night kiss at the door."

Padraig had actually been the one to set Colm up with Brooke a couple months earlier. His brother had taken Brooke out a few years ago, but the dating ended the night he met Mia. After that, Padraig was a goner, falling fast and furious, for his beautiful future wife. Padraig had always been the king of love at first sight, but Colm had to admit, with Mia, his brother hadn't been wrong.

"Well, I guess it's a safe bet that you, the last of the original gigolos, have done more than just kiss the girl."

Colm leaned back, adopting a cocky pose. "Let's just say I'm rounding the bases at a steady pace. Always was a better ballplayer than Paddy."

Kelli snorted. "Rounding the bases, huh? No home run. Sounds like you're slowing down in your old age."

"You don't have to worry about that happening. Ever. That scoreboard's about to change. Brooke and I have made after-party plans for Halloween. I'm going to spend the night at her place."

"Well, she's definitely your type."

"I have a type?"

"Don't be thick, Colm. Of course you do. Blonde, bubbly, more cute than pretty, boobs a must, but brains optional."

Colm considered that, then smiled. "Damn. I do have a type. You realize *you* have a type too."

She shook her head. "No, I don't. I'm open-minded."

"Bullshit. You go for wimps, guys you can run roughshod over and control."

"There's absolutely nothing wrong with sensitive men, guys who actually have souls, and who don't look at women and only see a nice pair of tits and a firm ass."

"Maybe not, but I guarantee none of those men have ever rocked your world in bed."

He got the sense his words had struck a chord when she didn't reply right away. It seemed as if it took her a second to regroup.

Interesting.

Maybe he was wrong about Kelli's type.

"My sex life is just fine. Or...it was...when I had one."

He shook his head, as if disappointed. "Just fine? Wow. What a terrible description. You ever been tied up in bed, Kell? Spanked? Had your hair pulled?"

Kelli rolled her eyes, her usual response to pretty much everything he said to her, but this time, it felt more like a dodge than a reaction.

"So you haven't," he pressed.

"I'm not discussing my sex life with you, perv."

"That's all the answer I need. Pity. I think you'd get off on a little bondage."

She leaned toward him, lowering her voice, the sound surprising husky...sexy. "I think I would."

Colm's eyes widened, and he shifted closer as well, always ready to go tit for tat with her. "Oh yeah? Should you and I test that theory?" It wasn't a serious offer, and Kelli knew it.

And her answer was exactly what he'd expected. "As long as I'm the one tying the knots."

He chuckled. "Yet another reason why you and I will never hook up."

"Jesus, Colm. Believe me, that has never been in the cards. Ever. Like *never. Ever.*"

"Agreed. Want a cup of coffee to sober up?" he offered, though he made no effort to stand.

She shook her head. "No. That will just keep me up all night, and I'm perfectly capable of not sleeping on my own."

He saw her wince slightly before schooling her features,

and it set his lawyer instincts on full alert. Kelli had clearly revealed something she hadn't meant to.

And since it was his God-given duty as an attorney to question her, he did. "Something keeping you up nights? More than just cat puke, spilled coffee, and shitty pants?"

She shrugged casually.

Colm figured she'd brush his question off—but then she twisted on the couch and faced him more fully.

"I've been...thinking about something...and I..."

She paused, and he recognized the second she realized who she was talking to. "You and Paddy really do look alike with the beard. Keep forgetting he shaved his off."

Colm chuckled. "Almost spilled your guts to me, didn't you?"

Kelli didn't share the laugh. Instead, she shocked him by asking, "Would you give me shit until the end of time if I did?"

Colm wasn't sure how to respond. He and Kelli had a pretty solid frenemies schtick, something that had worked for them since they were kids. But there was something in her tone that...worried him.

"I won't give you shit."

She studied his face, but his tone must have convinced her he was sincere. "I considered talking to Paddy about this, but...this doesn't feel like something I can..."

She kept stopping in the middle of her sentences, as if she was still debating with herself over opening up to him.

"There's something you can't tell Paddy?" Colm was fairly certain there'd never been anything in their entire lives that had been off-limits between Kelli and Padraig.

"You know how hard the holidays are on him."

Colm nodded. Of course he knew that. Just like he knew there were several other times during the year that knocked his brother down as well, times that had been meaningful, special to him and Mia. March, the month they'd met, was particularly brutal for Padraig.

Padraig and Mia had only gotten to spend one Christmas together. One lousy holiday, but Padraig had done everything in his power to make it the greatest holiday season ever —from Halloween, to Thanksgiving, to Christmas, and New Year's, he'd made every single day the perfect celebration, the perfect memory.

And he'd paid for it the last two years. The holidays never failed to kick his brother in the ass. Hard.

"So it's just the holidays holding you back from talking to him?"

Kelli considered the question, then shook her head. "No. It's the subject matter too. I don't know if...I'm not sure he'd understand. He's kind of a romantic."

"Kind of? Jesus. That's the understatement of the year."

"Yeah. It is. So there's no way he'd get what I'm planning."

Colm turned on the couch, resting his arm against the back cushions. "What the hell are you going to do? Shave your head? Join a cult? Marry your cat? Now you *have* to tell me."

He expected her to flip him off. Or even to rise and walk upstairs. They weren't confidants. Not even close to that.

Once again, she didn't follow their usual pattern.

Instead...she answered. "I'm thirty-four."

"I'm well aware. We're the same age, remember? I was the one who cut your Barbie doll's hair off in kindergarten."

She narrowed her eyes. "Forgot about that. Damn, you were a dick right from the cradle."

"The Barbie haircut was retaliation for the hole you poked in my soccer ball."

"Ohhhh yeahhhhh."

Colm scowled. "It was a brand-new ball."

"You pulled my hair. It hurt."

"Bet you wouldn't bitch about getting your hair pulled these days."

She blew out an exasperated breath. "Oh my God. Get your mind out of the gutter, Collins."

He and Kelli were almost exactly the same age, he and Padraig only five weeks older. They'd all three celebrated their birthdays together last summer. "Fine, so you're thirty-four. What's the problem with that?"

"I'm out of time."

Colm tilted his head, totally confused. "For what?"

"Children. My clock is ticking."

Colm shook his head. "I'm sure a woman's clock doesn't start ticking until—"

"Thirty-two."

"I thought it was thirty-five."

Kelli shook her head. "Nope. It starts at thirty-two."

"Oh. Well. Shit."

"Yeah. Oh. Well. Shit," she repeated.

He tried to minimize her concerns, certain things weren't as dire as she thought. "Come on, Kell. You're hardly ancient. I'm sure..."

"Did you know fertility drops rapidly after the age of 35?"

Colm winced, hoping to make her laugh. "Do you have to use words like fertility around me?"

She turned away from him, flopping her head back against the couch cushions. "I have no idea why I started this conversation with you."

Damn. It was no wonder the two of them didn't spend time alone together. After so many years of teasing and insults, he was saying all the wrong things simply because it was too hard to break the pattern.

Feeling guilty, he took a deep breath and tried again. "You know, there are a ton of kids in the foster care system who are looking for good homes. You could talk to Aunt Lauren about it."

His aunt Lauren, Uncle Sean and Uncle Chad had taken in a few foster kids over the years, including Gavin, who was now sharing this apartment with him, sleeping down the hall.

"I've considered that. And maybe that's something I'll do as well, but...I want the experience, want to be pregnant, to feel a life growing inside me. I can't imagine anything more...amazing."

Colm nodded. "Yeah. I want to be a dad too. Someday. In the far, far future."

Kelli grimaced. "Still hanging on to your vow of not settling down until your forties?"

"Still a lot of women who haven't gotten to enjoy an evening in my bed. Hate to take myself off the market too soon."

"On behalf of my gender, let me just reassure you...none of us would lose any sleep at night over that sale ending. And let's face it, you have the luxury of waiting as long as you want. You can make babies at any age."

Colm considered her point of view, her concerns. "I understand why you're telling me and not Paddy, Kell. You and I have lived parallel lives when it comes to our dating histories. Neither one of us has ever been particularly lucky at love. Everyone in my family gets the fairy tale ending, while you and I stand on the sidelines and watch."

"Paddy didn't exactly get the fairy tale ending."

"No. I guess he didn't."

"And you're right. I love your family, Colm, but damn if they don't make things tough on us mere mortals. I've spent too many years around people who've found the most amazing, beautiful true loves, while I seem to be a magnet for losers."

He could completely relate to that. "Which makes it harder when you're still alone night after night."

She studied his face. "You do get it."

He nodded slowly. "I get it." Painfully so, though he didn't add that part.

"That's why I'm done, Colm. I'm taking my hat out of the ring. Giving up on the dating scene."

"I don't understand how taking yourself out of the dating scene will solve the ticking clock issue," he said, struggling to connect the dots. "Those two things don't go together."

"I don't need a boyfriend or a husband to have a baby."

Colm frowned. "What do you mean?"

"I'm going to have a baby. On my own."

Colm gave her a crooked grin. "Hate to break it to you, but I'm fairly certain no human is capable of parthenogenesis. There's this little thing called the sperm."

Kelli smacked his arm. "I know that, asshole. But there's also this little thing called a sperm donor."

Jesus. Kelli was batting a thousand on the shocks tonight. "You'd seriously go that route?"

She sucked in a deep breath. "Yeah. I would. I've been thinking about it a lot this past year. Like *a lot*. I want to have a baby, Colm."

"So what are we talking here? Turkey baster or something?"

She laughed. "Crude. But yeah, something like that. This isn't some spur-of-the-moment decision. I've considered everything. Budgeting, childcare, my living situation. I have a plan for all of it. I know I can do this."

"Yeah, but a sperm donor? You can't get pregnant like that. I mean, what are you talking about? Going to a sperm bank and picking out some swimmers based on...Jesus. Based on what?" Colm wasn't sure why her plan bothered him so much. It was none of his business, and it wasn't like he didn't believe Kelli would be a great mother, single or not. She'd be fantastic at it.

Sometimes he wondered if her still-single status had something to do with the fact she was an extremely strong, independent, speak-her-mind woman. Colm figured there were probably a lot of guys who would be intimidated by that.

He didn't fall into that category, but that was because he'd grown up surrounded by women just like her, and there was no way his mother, aunts, and female cousins wouldn't have kicked his ass from here to Iceland if he'd revealed any caveman-like attitudes.

"A sperm bank is an option, but I don't really want to go

that route. Ideally, I'd like to at least know the guy. I mean, you know my girlfriends, Lydia and Kristen—"

"The lipstick lesbians?"

"You know, when you say stupid shit like that, it—"

"Okay, okay," he said with a grin. Kelli was friends with two of the hottest women on the planet, so it had really rocked his world when his flirting was rebuffed. His ego had taken a major hit until Kelli let him off the hook and told him why he'd never stood a chance. "Believe me, I know exactly who they are. A loss for our team," he mumbled, enjoying the way she narrowed her eyes at him. It was so easy to get a rise out of her.

"After they got married, they decided they wanted to have a kid. Lydia asked a guy she'd grown up with if he would donate the sperm. She knew his family history, knew him, plus he's a hot orthodontist, smart, funny, the whole package."

"And he just gave them sperm and walked away? Gave up all rights to the kid?"

"For one thing, he's married and lives in Iowa, and I'm sure he'll see the kid on occasion, but you're looking at this the wrong way. That's not the point."

"What *is* the point?"

"The point is, Lydia and Kristen are the parents. He just gave them...a gift."

"Of sperm? You know most people give Keurigs or place settings as wedding gifts. Not sure I've ever seen sperm on a registry."

"I hate you."

Colm smiled. "I know."

"I don't even know why I started this conversation with you. Forget I said anything."

"No. I don't want to forget it. I'm glad you're telling me. And I meant what I said. I do understand."

She tilted her head.

"Always so suspicious," he teased.

"I considered talking to Sunnie or Yvonne or Darcy, but they're all so...emotional, driven by true love and all that shit."

"Yep. The Collins curse is real." For years, he'd sworn the Collinses had lived under a curse and, when it struck, it caused the person afflicted to fall in love fast and hard. It had been a joke for a while, but as more and more of his cousins found their soul mates, there was no denying the curse was real.

Though God knew none of those struck by it considered it a curse at all. His cousin Lochlan, the last man he'd ever expected to succumb to marriage, called it a blessing.

"So you're considering a sperm bank, but you'd rather get the," he finger-quoted, "'gift sperm' from a guy you know, someone you choose."

She nodded. "I've been working on a list, but it's pretty damn skimpy."

"Oh yeah? Who's on it?"

She shook her head. "None of your business."

"We know a lot of the same people, Kell. Maybe I can help you narrow down your options. Am I on it?"

"Fuck no!"

"What? That's a mistake." He flexed his muscles for her. "You gotta want these genes."

"Pass. Hard pass."

Colm shrugged in a *your loss* way, then he had an unsettling thought. "Is Paddy on the list?"

"He was originally, but no. I marked his name out."

"Why?"

"You know why. He's not like that orthodontist in Iowa. He'd never walk away. *Never.* Besides, he's not moving on, and I'm scared he'll never get over Mia's death. If I asked him to do this, my fear is he would say yes, and then he'd give his whole life to the kid as another way to avoid getting out there and taking a chance on finding love and happiness again."

Colm nodded. "You're right. He would. So who's on the list?"

"Robbie Pullman."

"Why is that name familiar?"

"You've probably heard me mention him before. The two of us went to college together. Dated for a hot minute. We run into each other occasionally and we're friendly."

"What makes this guy a contender?" Colm asked.

"He teaches high school science here at one of the local magnet schools. He's a super-nice guy, extremely intelligent, good-looking. I haven't managed to dig too deep into his family medical history yet, but—"

"Wait. You've already talked to him about this?"

Kelli nodded. "Yeah."

"And what did he say?"

"He was flattered. Said he needed to think about it, but he didn't say no. Actually, the more we talked, the more I started to think he was leaning toward yes."

Colm rubbed his beard, trying to wrap his head around Kelli getting pregnant, becoming a mother. There was actually a tiny part of him that was almost jealous. Not of

Robbie, but of her. He hadn't really considered becoming a dad yet, as he was still trying to find the woman he'd like to be the mother, but now...she'd planted a seed. "Are you really sure about this, Kelli? Have you thought it all through?"

She nodded. "I've spent the last year thinking of very little else. I don't have any problem doing this or doing it alone. I really don't. I have enough love to be both parents—the mom and the dad. I want a child so bad, Colm, and at this point, well, when you factor in the whole meet someone, fall in love, get married timeline..."

"It could be a whirlwind romance."

She blew out a hard breath. "Yeah. Because I haven't been looking for one of *those* the last fifteen years. They're not as easy to come by as you might think. Unless you're a Collins, of course."

"Well, of course," he joked, then he studied her face. "Never really thought of you as a mom, but...I can see it," he said, grinning widely. "Though you're going to have to cut back on your wine consumption and use of the word fuck. Hmmm...talk about entering uncharted territory."

"I'll be just fine," she said sarcastically. "And please don't overwhelm me with your confidence."

"Tell you what. Why don't you invite Robbie to the Halloween party so I can check him out? See if he meets our high level of standards."

"*Our* standards?" Kelli asked. "Oh no, Colm Collins. You get no say in this."

"Invite him anyway. Call it curiosity."

Kelli started to shake her head, and he realized she probably thought he was up to something.

He raised his right hand. "I swear I just want to meet the guy. See what's so hot about his sperm."

Kelli laughed. "Is this a jealousy thing? Are you pissed off that I don't want yours?"

Was he?

No. Absolutely not. While Kelli didn't say it—maybe she didn't even think it—he was concerned he might be a lot like Padraig in this situation. He wasn't sure he'd be able to walk away from any child that was his. Gift sperm or not.

"I'm not pissed off about that. I just want to meet him. Is that such a big deal? Besides, you should want him to meet my family."

"Why?" she asked.

"Because I noticed when you listed his attributes, you didn't mention his sense of humor or ability to have fun. I think those things should rank pretty high on your genetics list."

"So you're a nature-over-nurture guy? You don't think I can raise a fun-loving kid? Seriously?"

Colm knew without a doubt any child reared by Kelli would have an awesome sense of humor.

"Although," she said, tapping her finger on her lips, "that actually isn't a bad test to run. Besides, when he sees me win the costume contest, he'll realize how incredibly awesome I am, and I bet he agrees then and there to be my sperm donor."

"You're not winning the contest this year. I'm going balls to the wall."

Kelli shrugged as if unconcerned. "I think you forget who you're talking to. I'm currently the record holder in terms of wins."

"Bullshit. We're tied at three each, and you know it."

"Fuck off," Kelli said. "I'm not having the Baron Samedi debate with you again. You cheated that year."

Colm shook his head, fighting like the devil to hide his smile. "Kelli, Kelli, Kelli, there is such a thing as a sore loser."

"Nope. Not a sore loser. You found out what my costume was going to be—something I'll never forgive Paddy for—and—"

"In his defense, he just asked me who Baron Samedi was. I figured out why he was asking on my own."

"And then came as the same thing. Your whole family thought we'd planned it."

"And crowned us *both* the winners. A tie."

"I wore it better. Sunnie even said so, and since it wasn't a planned," she air quoted, "'partner costume,' I was the winner because it was my awesome idea. So I have three wins to your two."

Colm let the debate end there, simply because they'd already had this fight approximately forty-two thousand times since that Halloween. He let his casual shrug tell her he wasn't conceding. "Doesn't matter. This year, I've got it in the bag. My family might even decide it's the greatest costume of all time and stop holding the contest altogether since it'll never be topped."

"We'll see." Then she glanced at her phone and winced. "It's after one, Colm."

He groaned as he pushed himself up from the couch. "Tomorrow is not going to be fun."

Kelli followed him to the kitchen as he grabbed both of them a bottle of water, then they locked up, turned out the lights, and headed for the stairs.

When they reached the top, she stopped at the threshold to Finn's room, watching as Colm continued to his door. Once he was there, he turned back to look at her.

"Night, Kell."

"Night," she repeated. "And, Colm, thanks."

He nodded and smiled before walking into his room and closing the door, trying to recall if Kelli Peterson had ever thanked him for anything before.

Then he tried to remember if he'd ever done anything worthy of her thanks.

That thought provoked a chuckle...until he shed his clothes and flopped down onto his bed.

Kelli wanted a baby.

Those words drifted through his mind as he closed his eyes, lulled to sleep by the image of him holding his own baby in his arms, rocking the little thing to sleep.

It was peaceful and perfect.

Until he realized Kelli was there too.

What the fuck was that about?

"Too much Guinness," he murmured just before he fell asleep.

CHAPTER THREE

Kelli laughed once again when Colm walked—or more accurately, stomped—by her in his Hagrid costume. The man had actually bought platform boots that added at least six more inches to his already six-foot-four height.

When she and Robbie had first arrived at the Collins Dorm for the Halloween party, it had taken her close to five minutes to figure out it was Colm in the costume. The majority of his face was hidden beneath a shaggy beard and wig, and he'd added quite a bit of padding under the long, tattered trench coat. No part of the well-dressed lawyer was present tonight, and though it killed her to admit it, he looked so much like the character, it was uncanny.

"I'm going to grab another beer," Robbie said, pointing toward the kitchen where the keg was. "Want anything?"

She lifted her wineglass. "Nope, I'm good. Just refilled. Something I'm going to pay for tomorrow." She really did need to get a grip on her wine consumption. She was out of control this week.

Oh, who was she fooling? This decade.

Robbie grinned. "We're celebrating."

"Damn right we are," she said with a laugh as he walked away.

"What are you celebrating? You lost the costume contest, Merida," Colm said, somehow managing to sneak up on her from behind, a pretty amazing feat considering he really wasn't very quiet in those boots.

God only knew what the patrons of Pat's Pub below thought was going on up here. Colm's dad, Tris, had come up earlier to ask if they were using a jackhammer on the floor. He'd taken one look at Colm's costume, rolled his eyes, muttered "competitive bastard" under his breath, and gone right back downstairs.

She'd been so sure she would take first prize this year. She had the hair, the dress, the bow and arrows, everything just perfect for her favorite Scottish Disney princess. She'd worn the costume to school yesterday, and her kids had gone out of their little minds. Of course, it helped that she had long red hair and they constantly told her she looked just like Merida.

Kelli narrowed her eyes at Lucas and Caitlyn, this year's costume contest winners. "They had a very unfair advantage."

Colm chuckled. "You're not kidding. But you have to admit that costume was a pretty awesome way to tell the family she's pregnant."

Colm's cousin and partner at the Collins and Collins law

firm, Caitlyn, had shown up with her husband, the two of them dressed as Daddy and Mommy Shark, while Caitlyn had pinned a stuffed shark to the front of her shirt with a note attached that read "Baby Shark arriving in April."

"You really didn't know she was pregnant?" Kelli asked.

"No. And I fully intend to read her the riot act for that at work on Monday."

Kelli could tell from Colm's tone that he would do no such thing. He and Caitlyn were very close, and while she couldn't see much of his face, she could tell he was beyond happy for his cousin.

He lifted one leg. "I'm just glad Sunnie awarded the prize early. I'm done with these boots. They're killing my feet."

Kelli lifted her dress to reveal her bare feet. "I kicked off my heels two seconds after she pronounced Caitlyn and Lucas the winners." She pointed to where she'd shucked them into a corner. "Wanna add to my pile?"

He nodded. "Yeah. I'll do that in a second. You didn't tell me what you're celebrating."

Kelli's smile widened as she rose up on tiptoe and leaned as close to Colm's ear as she could manage. "Robbie said yes. We went to dinner before the party and talked some more. He's in on the *you know what*."

Colm nodded, but she couldn't tell if he was smiling or not, thanks to the damn bushy beard. Something in his eyes made her think he wasn't happy for her, which bothered her more than she cared to consider. He'd really seemed to get it the other night. So much so, she'd slept like a baby—granted, the wine had probably helped—for the first time in months.

She sure as hell hadn't intended to confide her hope for a baby to Colm, but the fact he'd been supportive had gone a long way toward setting her mind at ease.

Mainly because she knew there were more than enough people in her life—her mother, primarily—who weren't going to get it, and who were going to make damn sure she knew it.

Her concerns were washed away after his next question.

"So...when is he going to transfer the funds?" Colm asked.

The fact that Kelli laughed proved she'd had too much damn wine tonight. "Really, Colm? Transfer the funds?"

He chuckled. "You want me to come up with some other way to describe it? Because I'm sure if I put my mind to it, I could—"

"No. Please. Spare me. We going to do it over Christmas break, mid-December."

"Damn. That's soon."

Kelli shook her head. "Not really. Now that he's said yes, I'm sort of wondering if I should push it up. Don't want him to change his mind, now that it's decided." She glanced over at Caitlyn and felt the strongest pang of...desire. It sounded cliché, but Caitlyn really did glow.

Kelli couldn't wait to be pregnant.

"She's really happy," Colm observed, clearly looking at his cousin as well. "Not sure I've ever seen her that happy, and she's been pretty obnoxiously in love with Lucas for nearly four years."

"Obnoxiously in love. Yeah. That's a great description. For pretty much everyone in this room right now," Kelli said, looking around.

The apartment was packed with the Collins family and their friends. Sunnie, the party planner, was reloading the pigs-in-a-blanket platter with help from her husband, Landon. Finn was scrolling through the music selections with his partners, Layla and Miguel. Fergus and Aubrey were slow dancing in a corner to a song apparently only the two of them could hear, considering the upbeat, fast tune that was currently filling the apartment.

On and on it went. Yvonne and Leo were there, as well as Hunter and Ailis, Lochlan and May. Every corner of the room was occupied by Colm's cousins, all of them with their significant others, dancing, laughing, talking.

Being obnoxiously in love.

Kelli shook off her sudden melancholy and pushed it down deep. Then she heard Colm's loud sigh and realized, in this room surrounded by happy lovers, they had something in common.

God help her. This was what life had come to. She now had a kindred spirit in Colm.

Fuck.

Looking around the room again, she spotted Robbie and Brooke in the kitchen, talking as he poured a beer from the keg.

"Your sperm donor is putting the moves on my date," Colm muttered.

Kelli pointed to his pink umbrella. "You're the one with the wand. Expelliarmus his ass."

Colm laughed.

"You know, it's a shame Brooke didn't get the word that this was a costume contest," Kelli teased.

Colm snorted. "Don't be catty, Kell. I think she's rocking

the Regina George look. I like the tight pink sweater. Really accentuates her..." He held his hands out in front of his chest like he was carrying invisible melons, letting her fill in the blanks.

She snorted. "Like I said the other night. Just your type. Big tits. Brain optional."

"Brooke's brain is just fine. I mean...she's not the most stimulating conversationalist, but she's nice enough, and I've now had a complete rundown of the last season of *The Bachelor*. It was a nail biter. Should I catch you up?"

Kelli made a horrified face. "I'll pass on the recap. Thanks anyway. So...are you still planning on rounding the rest of the bases?"

"Oh yeah. Hagrid is getting laid tonight."

"Please," she said, holding up her hand. "I don't need the kinky *Harry Potter*, *Mean Girls* visual. I just ate."

Colm spun his umbrella wand like a baton. "You're just jealous."

"And you're a slut."

He pulled her hair, winking suggestively, reminding her of his questions the other night about her sexual experiences. Last night, she'd actually spent a little time with her vibrator, her sexy fantasy one of bondage and a spanking and even the hairpulling. She'd come harder than she had in a very long time.

Until she realized Colm had been the man in the fantasy.

Then every loosey-goosey, happy feeling evaporated and she'd gotten up to take a cold shower, trying to forget about it.

She wasn't sure she'd be able to pull that fantasy out

again in the future. She was too afraid of a repeat performance. The last thing she needed was to start thinking about Colm as anything other than her lifelong frenemy.

"You sure you want to go the turkey baster route? I bet Han Solo wouldn't mind pulling his lightsaber out for you."

Kelli glanced back at Robbie, who had now been shanghaied into helping Sunnie add more ice to the keg bucket. She had to admit he was passing her Collins test with flying colors, able to hang with the crazy, fun-loving family easily.

"First of all, Han Solo doesn't have a lightsaber. He has a blaster."

"Even better," Colm interjected, but she ignored him.

"This isn't about sex, Colm. I want a baby. Not Robbie. He's a nice guy, but we tried the dating thing and it didn't work. Just like it hasn't worked with the other three-thousand, nine-hundred and forty-two guys I've gone out with since high school."

"That thing with Robbie was in college. Maybe he's gotten better in bed."

Kelli groaned. "You have a one-track mind. He and I never slept together. And I told you, I'm taking myself out of the meat market."

"So you're never going out with another man?"

"No. That's not what I'm saying. I'm just not waiting for Prince Charming to arrive and sweep me off my feet. I've finally realized that me going for what I truly want—"

"A baby," he added.

"Isn't tied to me having a ring on my finger. This isn't an all-or-nothing proposition."

"Yeah, but it's going to be a heck of a lot harder to date with a kid. You know that, right?"

"Seriously, Colm? Is the male ego so large and so fragile that it can't stand up to an independent, single mother?"

"Of course not."

"Oh, okay, so if it's not that, then I guess I'm supposed to cave to some archaic societal stricture that says a woman has to wait for marriage before she can become a mother because the poor, simple-minded female couldn't possibly raise a child on her own. Is that right?"

"You're putting words in my mouth that I'm not saying."

"Are you thinking them?"

He paused, then—wise man—he shook his head. "No. I'm not. I meant what I said the other night, Kelli. You'll be a great mom, and I know you're perfectly capable of doing it on your own."

"It'll probably be easier without a man," she grumbled.

He chuckled. "Probably."

She gave him a rueful, apologetic smile. "Sorry. I guess you can tell I'm sort of gearing myself up to defend my decision against the naysayers. There are going to be plenty of people in my life—other friends, colleagues at work, my mother—who are going to feel it's their God-given right to express their opinion about how I should live my life."

"You can blame social media for that. Just remember, it's your decision, your life. If anyone doesn't agree, just say fuck 'em."

"You've met my mother, Colm. Do you seriously think that's going to work?"

Colm didn't bother to hide his wince. "Maybe you shouldn't tell your mom until the kid's eighteen and off to college."

Kelli laughed. "Believe me, I've considered that." She

loved her mother, she really did. But her mother tested her. Frequently. Daily.

If a person looked up overbearing in the dictionary, Barb Peterson's picture would be there as the prime example. No doubt every teacher and principal Kelli ever had was glad to see the backside of her leaving their class or school forever, not because of anything *she* did, but because it meant they wouldn't have to deal with Barb anymore. Her mother was loud, brusque, narrow-minded, and demanding, and, as much as it shamed Kelli to admit, she'd spent her entire life completely mortified by the woman.

"Don't envy you that conversation," Colm said, and his tone was so serious, so kind, she knew he wasn't giving her shit. He was sincere.

"Thanks. I don't know how—"

Before she could continue, Padraig stumbled over, his speech slightly slurred. "Oh man. Who left you two alone together? Is everything okay over here? Do I need to ring the bell to end the round?"

"Wow. Bourbon much, Farmer Collins?" Kelli asked, when she caught a whiff of his breath.

Padraig rarely got drunk. In fact, Kelli could count the number of times on one hand, and four of those would have been in the weeks after Mia's death.

Tonight. He was...

"Jesus, Paddy," Colm said, scowling. "You're plastered."

Emmy stood next to him, looking absolutely adorable. She'd talked Padraig into doing a partner costume with her— something Kelli took the time to point out to Colm as a way of teaching him what a true partner costume looked like. Padraig was a farmer, while Emmy was a strawberry.

Emmy gave them a wry grin, obviously as taken aback by Padraig's current state as they were. "Apparently, he did some pregaming down at the pub with your Pop Pop before the party started."

"Shit, I'd say he pregamed, tailgated, day-drank through the game, *and* celebrated the triple overtime win. How about some water, Paddy?" Colm offered, intent on leading his brother to the kitchen.

"Nope. I'm having fun. Water will just kill my buzz."

"I'm not sure there's enough water in the world to do that," Kelli said. "But just for argument's sake, what do you say we give it a try?"

"Let me have that." Colm took Padraig's cup from him, sipping from it. "Jesus. Did you forget to add the Coke?"

"Coke is just there to add a splash of color," Padraig explained. "Give me my drink. I don't lecture *you* two when you knock 'em back at the pub for hours on end."

Kelli looked at Colm and shrugged. "He's right. He doesn't. So...Colm. We have a choice to make. Are we going to be the voice of reason or go to the next level with him?"

Colm rubbed his forehead. "I'm still suffering from leveling up with you on Wednesday. A one-day buffer in between isn't enough."

Kelli didn't reply. Just gave him a look that was pure dare.

"Fine. Where's your bottle of bourbon, Paddy?"

"I'll get it." Emmy stepped away then returned from the kitchen with half a fifth of bourbon, a couple cans of Coke, two more red Solo cups, and Robbie in tow. She started to hand one to Kelli, who shook her head.

"Fuck no. I'm good with the wine."

"I like bourbon," Robbie said, taking the extra cup.

Emmy played bartender for once, pouring each of the guys a drink, though she was more generous with the Coke than Padraig had been. Brooke joined them as the women lifted their wineglasses, the men their cups, and Colm issued his usual toast.

"Bottoms up. Especially yours."

"Hey," Sunnie said, crossing the room to Colm. "Where the hell is Darcy?"

Colm shrugged. "She texted me around seven and said she had to work a little late, but I thought she'd be here by now."

"I better call her and che—"

Sunnie stopped mid-sentence as the lights flickered and then went out completely.

The room, which had been filled with music and loud voices, was suddenly very quiet and pitch-black.

"What the hell?" Sunnie said.

Several people pulled out their cell phones and fired up the flashlight app. When a few minutes passed, it became pretty obvious the power wasn't coming back on.

Kelli made her way over to the window. "It's not just us. Looks like the whole street is out. It's dark as sin out there."

Everyone started talking at once because, as Kelli had learned a long time ago, that was how the Collins clan communicated. It had taken her quite a few years when she was younger to get the knack of talking and listening at the same time, but the skill had come in handy now that she was a kindergarten teacher.

Suddenly, a loud whistle cut through the noise and everyone fell silent again.

"Jesus, Sunnie. I think you pierced my eardrum," Landon said.

"Sorry," Sunnie said, without an ounce of remorse in her voice. "But they weren't quieting down for you."

Landon shook his head, then said, "Hey, listen up. It's a city-wide blackout. Transformer fire at a substation. They don't know how long the power will be out." Landon looked around. "Miguel? Where are you, man?"

"Over here," Miguel called out from a shadowy area near the dining room table.

"Aaron just called. They need us to go into work."

Miguel and Landon were both on the Baltimore police force, and Colm's uncle Aaron was their boss. Both of them had been drinking soda because every cop was officially "on call" on Halloween. As such, Kelli suspected every cop in the city was being called in at the moment. Blackouts were prime season for looting and God only knew what else in Baltimore. Add in the Halloween factor and chances were good shit could go south fast.

"Dammit," Sunnie grumbled, even as she gave Landon a quick kiss on the cheek. "Be careful."

Miguel and Landon shone themselves a path with the flashlights on their phones, making their way to the steps that led down to the pub.

Yvonne followed. "I'd better go help Dad sort things out with whoever is still dining on Sunday's Side."

"Oh yeah. The pub." Padraig started to follow her, but Colm put a hand on his chest to stop him.

"I need to help Dad, Colm."

"Yeah. I'm not sure how much help you'd be at the moment, Bro."

Mercifully, Finn emerged with Layla. "We'll go down and help Uncle Tris, Paddy. Why don't you stay up here and help Sunnie?"

Kelli walked over to Sunnie. "Want some help trying to clean up?"

"Clean up?" Sunnie asked. "The night is still young."

Kelli laughed. God. She should have known better than to assume a little thing like no lights or music would dim the festivities.

Ailis and Caitlyn had managed to round up a bunch of candles, lighting them, which created the perfect atmosphere for a spooky Halloween party.

"Okay, okay," Sunnie said, trying to get everyone's attention. When that failed, she stuck two fingers in the corners of her mouth again and pierced the air with another of her loud whistles. Kelli had asked Sunnie to teach her how to do that once, thinking it would come in handy on the playground at recess, but Kelli hadn't been able to produce the ear-splintering volume Sunnie was capable of.

Once everyone was quiet, Sunnie held up a bottle of tequila. "I've got an idea for an awesome game."

"Oh yeah. This is where the night takes a horrible, horrible turn," Colm muttered sarcastically and just loud enough for everyone to hear him.

"Oh ye of little faith, Colm," Sunnie chastised. "You all know the movie *A Quiet Place*, right?"

"I don't do scary movies," Ailis said.

Sunnie dismissed that. "Yeah, but you know the main gist of it, don't you?"

"You can't talk or the monsters kill you?" Ailis asked.

"Yes!" Sunnie was clearly excited about her plan. "Except in our game, I'm the monster and if I hear you, you have to take a shot of tequila."

"So you expect us to walk around here the rest of the night not talking?" Lochlan asked. Kelli practically heard the light bulb go on when Lochlan said, "I think I can get behind this game."

Lucas laughed and agreed. "Me too. Might go down as the best Collins party in history."

Caitlyn elbowed her husband. "You guys are only saying that because you think we're too loud."

"I just think this might prove once and for all," Lucas said, "that it is physically impossible for you Collins ladies to be together and not talking at top volume."

Caitlyn narrowed her eyes at her husband. "Twenty bucks says it's the men who drink the most shots by the end of the night."

And just like that, the betting and arguing over contest terms was on.

There was a longstanding argument between the male and female Collinses that the women talked too much and too loud. Of course, that wasn't the part the ladies debated. They insisted the men were just as loud and talked just as much.

Kelli had been around long enough that she'd chosen a side, residing firmly in the women's camp. She'd spent too many playdates with Padraig, Colm, and their other male cousins, Lochlan, Finn, Oliver, and Fergus, not to know exactly how loud they could get. Especially when it involved sports.

"That's not a fair contest. Not with Sunnie pouring the drinks. She'll only hear the men whispering," Fergus said.

"Agreed," Colm chimed in. "We need an impartial third party. Emmy, you don't have a horse in this race, right?"

Emmy laughed. "It's safe to say I think you're all insane, but no, I would have no problem handing out the shots fairly. Kind of like the idea of being a monster. Wish I'd known ahead of time. Paddy and I could have come as vampires or something."

"Damn. Missed opportunity," Padraig said, laughing, as he held his hands up like claws, adopting a Dracula accent. "I vant to suck your blood!"

Kelli couldn't help but grin. Padraig was actually a pretty funny drunk. She couldn't wait to tease him about this in the morning.

Once the wagers were placed—which took a ridiculous amount of time—Sunnie declared the game was on.

And just like that...silence.

For about thirty-two seconds. Which was how long it took for Padraig to ask Emmy if she'd seen his drink.

At which point, they all cracked up laughing, then started again.

Kelli was amazed by how well the game worked after that, and how much fun it was. They started using all the rooms in the apartment to hide and chat while Emmy, who nailed her role as the monster, lurked in the shadows, unseen until—boom! Tequila shot.

Kelli was equal parts amused and terrified. It was perfect. They'd been playing for nearly two hours and no one was getting tired of it. Of course, the power still wasn't on, so it wasn't like there were a lot of other options either.

She ran into Padraig in the tiny office. He still wasn't super quiet, but at least he was managing to whisper now. Mercifully, Emmy stopped "catching" him because he was already going to be hungover enough tomorrow.

Kelli couldn't help but wonder what was going through his head tonight.

"You okay?" she mouthed/whispered into his ear. Through the dim candlelight, she saw him nod.

"Just," he shrugged, "a bad day. Seamus broke off the leash this morning and ran. I lost sight of him for a few minutes. Found him, but it brought up some old memories and..."

He let Kelli fill in what he wasn't saying. Seamus had been Mia's dog, the sweet animal completely devoted to her. Since then, he'd been Padraig's constant companion. Padraig called him his sidekick and he loved the dog to distraction.

Kelli could only imagine the panic Padraig must have felt when Seamus was lost, and she didn't want to consider the day the dear dog passed away. Right now, Seamus was Padraig's strongest, most important connection to Mia, and if —God, when—he lost him, she worried how Padraig would react.

"I understand," she whispered. "I'm glad you found him."

Padraig nodded, his face clearing slowly, and he gave her a genuine smile. "I love you, Kell. You're so sweet."

"Said no one ever," she joked.

"You're my best friend. I couldn't live without you."

She knew it was the bourbon talking, so she rolled her eyes in an attempt not to show how much his words meant to her. "I love you too, you drunk lunatic."

He chuckled as he gave her a kiss on the cheek, and then they snuck out of the room, scanning the area for the monster.

A few minutes later, she ran into Robbie in Oliver's bedroom. He and Fergus had been silently laughing over Fergus's girlfriend having to take yet another shot. Aubrey was struggling to grasp the concept of whispering quietly.

Robbie tiptoed over to her, bending until his lips were at her ear. "Thanks for inviting me. What a great night."

Kelli smiled, twisting until it was her mouth at *his* ear. "I'm glad you came. And thanks for saying yes to the other thing."

Robbie's grin was huge and infectious. He was a nice guy and, for a moment, she tried to recall why exactly they hadn't worked out as a couple in college.

"I'm honored you asked." Then he, like Padraig, gave her a kiss on the cheek. She was batting a thousand on platonic pecks tonight.

Story of my life.

Robbie lifted his empty cup and pointed toward the kitchen. She nodded, and they quietly walked down the hall. Through the dim light in the living room, she saw Colm and Brooke leaving.

She smirked. At least someone was getting lucky tonight.

Which led to another thought. There was now an empty bedroom—and it had her name all over it. The wine—she'd had way too much again—as well as the screwdrivers Brooke had given her when her wine ran out, were making her sleepy and sluggish.

She leaned toward Robbie and whispered, "Too much

wine." She pointed above her head. "Might lie down a few minutes. Head spinning."

He nodded. "Going to play longer. I'll come up before I leave."

"Okay."

They'd driven to the party separately since Kelli had already made plans with Darcy to spend the night here. She'd intended to sleep on the couch, but there were still too many people playing that game, and God only knew when they'd call it quits.

She'd text Colm in the morning and tell him she had shanghaied his bed. He wouldn't care.

She stealthily made her way up to Colm's room. It was still dark, so she had to feel her way around. Her phone was in her purse, which she'd tucked away in a closet downstairs. She considered going back down for it, then thought screw it. She was too close to a bed and too damn tired.

She unzipped her dress, sucking in a deep, relieved breath. The corset part was snug, and as the night wore on, it had gotten more and more uncomfortable. It had a built-in bra, so as she pushed the gown over her hips, Kelli realized she was basically naked, only her panties remaining.

She didn't care.

She tossed the dress into the corner where she thought there might be a chair, then gingerly made her way to the bed. Sinking onto the soft mattress, she crawled under the covers and sighed blissfully.

Colm had a very soft bed.

Kelli closed her eyes, listening to the rush of white noise pulsing through her ears that told her she was going to have one heck of a headache tomorrow.

"Too much wine," she whispered to the empty room.

When her announcement was met with silence, another thought came to her, one that hurt as she spoke it aloud.

"Alone again."

CHAPTER FOUR

Colm went back up to the Collins Dorm with Brooke and without the vodka they'd gone down to the pub for. She'd been drinking screwdrivers all night, and she'd run out of liquor. Colm had figured that was probably a good thing since they'd both over-imbibed, but Brooke had found Padraig and asked if they could "borrow" some from the pub.

His brother had said yes and offered to go get it, but Colm didn't want his drunk twin staggering behind the counter, surrounded by all that glass.

He'd offered to go, and Brooke had followed, as he led the way using the flashlight on his almost-dead cell phone. Once they were alone in the pub, Brooke had taken advantage of the ability to finally talk, giving him a rapid play-by-play of the game from her perspective. He hadn't bothered to mention he'd pretty much been there for the whole thing—and it had suddenly occurred to him, he'd really enjoyed the last couple of hours because it had been peaceful.

Brooke could talk.

A lot.

A fucking lot.

Once he'd had the bottle in hand, he'd rounded the counter, where Brooke waited for him. She'd stopped him with a hand on his chest, lifting her face to his. He'd placed the vodka and his phone on the bar and tugged her closer, attempting a kiss, but his beard was in the way. Brooke didn't appear to care about that when her hands drifted from his chest to his hips, pulling him closer and letting him know she was ready to move this party to the next level.

"Let's go upstairs," he'd murmured, ready to shed his damn costume.

"Okay," she'd whispered back.

Colm had picked up his phone and left the vodka on the bar.

Once they'd returned to the living room, he'd started to direct her to the second set of stairs that would lead to his bedroom.

They'd originally planned to go back to her place after the party, but both of them had consumed way too much, and with the blackout, Colm wasn't sure he wanted to attempt to grab an Uber and make his way across the too-dark city to her apartment. His room would be just fine.

They were at the foot of the steps when Sunnie stopped him.

"Tap on the keg is jacked up. Can you fix it?" she whispered. "I'd ask Paddy, but..."

She didn't bother to finish that sentence.

Colm nodded, then looked at Brooke. "I'll meet you in my room." He added, "Second door on the left," at the same time Emmy stepped out of the shadows and did her hilarious monster growl.

Shit. Busted. Again.

He took the tequila shot as Brooke made her way upstairs.

Colm followed Sunnie to the kitchen to fix the tap. Two twists and the thing shot beer straight into his face like a geyser.

"Shit!" he cursed loudly. Emmy appeared, but he shot her a look that said he was *not* paying the penalty when she walked in, tequila bottle raised.

She giggled at the sight of his fake beard, dripping with beer, and left again.

"Fucking wig and beard," he grumbled, taking them off and tossing them onto the kitchen counter.

"Oh my God. You and Paddy are twins again!" Sunnie whispered, reaching up to touch his clean-shaven cheek.

"Not for long. I'm growing the beard back again tomorrow. Couldn't get the Hagrid one to stick to my face with my own beard in the way." He'd shaved it off just before the party when he got sick of fucking around with the glue. Oliver had laughed his ass off when he saw what he'd done, proclaiming Colm was going too far just to win a costume contest. Colm had shaken his head and joked that Oliver must have been switched at birth because no true Collins would question his dedication to winning, no matter the cost.

Sunnie obviously *was* a Collins through and through because she merely gave him a look that said she wouldn't have expected anything less from him. "It really was an amazing costume. You would have won if not for..."

"Baby shark."

"Yeah. That was awesome."

Colm tucked away Sunnie's compliment about his costume, ready to bring it out to razz Kelli with at a later date.

He'd kicked off the platform boots a couple hours earlier, changing into a pair of comfortable tennis shoes. Shrugging off the padded trench coat, he sighed, glad to be out of the heavy thing and able to move again.

He tackled the tap again and managed to fix it. Leaving his costume in the kitchen, he headed upstairs with two things on his mind.

Sex, then sleep.

He'd just walked into his bedroom when he remembered his phone was in the pocket of the trench coat. He tried to see Brooke through the darkness, but the room was pitch-black. He couldn't even see his hand in front of his face. For a moment, he considered going down to grab his phone, just for the light.

"It's me," he whispered, but he got no response.

Fuck it. He didn't need light for sex. He knew where all the important parts were.

A slight rustle in the bed told him Brooke was already lying down and ready to go. They'd gone out a dozen or so times in the past few months, but neither of them was interested in jumping from casual dating to a full-blown relationship. Brooke had admitted over dinner earlier in the evening that she wasn't looking for anything serious at the moment. According to her, all she wanted was "a good time with no strings."

Colm could definitely handle the good time. And no strings was his preferred state of being.

Or at least, it used to be. Before Kelli started talking about babies, and he'd starting to think maybe his "good times" weren't that much fun anymore.

Nope. Not going there, he decided as he carefully made his way to the bed. He rummaged through his nightstand drawer quietly, pulling out a couple of condoms so they'd be easily accessible when they got to that point.

Tugging off his T-shirt and jeans, he crawled into the bed in only his boxers, sliding next to Brooke, who remained still.

As he wrapped his arms around her bare waist, he realized she'd fallen sound asleep.

He hadn't left her alone *that* long.

He was just tired enough that he considered rolling over and going to sleep himself.

"Are we doing this?" he barely whispered, when he thought he felt her stir.

She came awake slowly, and he wondered if she'd heard his question.

Then, he heard her breathless gasp, and it sounded for a second like she'd forgotten where she was.

Colm leaned closer. He could take care of that. Could remind her *exactly* where she was.

Get ready for a good time, he thought.

He pressed his lips to hers.

At first, hers were still as he kissed her, and he briefly wondered about her hesitance. Brooke was the one who'd initially invited him back to her place, and there'd been no question what she'd intended for them to do there.

His concern drifted away when her lips softened against his, and she started kissing him back.

Kissing without the Hagrid beard was much better.

He pressed her lips apart, touching her tongue with his. She tasted like orange juice and vodka. It was tangy and sweet and nice.

She lifted her arms, wrapping them around his neck. Like him, she'd stripped off most of her clothing before crawling into bed. He liked her lack of shyness. She'd come to his bed knowing what she wanted. Her bare breasts pressed against his chest, and he couldn't resist touching them.

They broke the kiss briefly as he grasped one of her breasts in his hand. She started to speak, but he placed his finger against her lips.

"Shhh."

It was all he said, but he felt her lips tip up in a smile, and then she fell silent. The game they'd begun downstairs was still in effect.

He kissed her again, squeezing her breast until she gasped, arching her back, encouraging him to do it again.

Colm took her nipple between his fingers and lightly pinched the tight nub, loving the tiny moan of pleasure his touch provoked. She was so damn responsive and hot. He repeated the same on her other breast as she ran her hands through his hair, closing her fists and tugging, pulling his head back so that she could lift her head and...

His cock twitched, then thickened, as she bit his jaw. She *seriously* sank her teeth in.

It hurt, but damn if he didn't fucking love it.

So it's like that.

She wanted something rougher, something wilder.

Jesus. He hadn't felt like he and Brooke were really a matched set until that moment.

They'd made out a few times, indulged in some pretty heavy petting. Regardless of that, it had all been pretty... well...run-of-the-mill, lackluster.

This felt different, exciting. He wasn't sure if it was the liquor or if they'd turned some sort of corner, but he wasn't going to question it.

He was all in.

He lowered his head to her shoulder and bit her in return. Her hips thrust upwards, toward him in response, and it was all he could do not to strip off her panties and his boxers and give in to her upspoken request.

He took a deep breath and reined it in, wanting to draw this out.

Her breathing grew heavier, more labored, when he ran his hand along her side, enjoying her slight shiver. Then he shifted his face lower and took one of her nipples into his mouth.

He groaned as her fingers pulled his hair even harder, his scalp burning as she held him to her. He increased the suction on her nipple, giving her the same pleasure laced with pain. She writhed beneath him, not to escape but as if she simply couldn't restrain herself.

He kept sucking, nipping, licking, loving her little squeaks and moans. He hadn't realized how much he relied on words in the bedroom, until now, when they'd tacitly agreed to take talking off the table.

Instead of telling him what he was doing to her, she was showing him through body language and with those adorable sighs.

He had no idea how long he played with her breasts. Time seemed to have no meaning tonight, and Colm was in no hurry to rush to the next part.

The same couldn't be said for Brooke, who was using her grip on his hair now in an attempt to pull him back over her. He sensed her unspoken pleas but responded with only a shake of the head. He wasn't finished playing with her. Not by a long shot.

He'd joked around with Kelli the other night about preferring his swinging single lifestyle, but in truth, he hadn't been with a woman in over eight months. He wasn't sure what to chalk that dry spell up to, other than long work hours and a lack of interest in any of the women he'd dated. Brooke had lasted the longest, mainly because she didn't put any demands on him or want more than he did. If they were both free, they went out. If not, no harm, no foul.

Grasping her wrists, he pulled her hands away from his hair, drawing them down to the pillow beneath her head. He pressed them firmly, telling her without words that he wanted her to leave them there. When he released her, he felt her lift them once more, her fingers only barely grazing his cheeks before he recaptured and returned them to the spot he wanted them, his grip tighter, more forceful.

When he released her this time, she didn't move her hands.

God, he wished he'd gone back for his phone or had thought to grab one of the candles. He longed to see her, wanted to see her body flush with arousal, wanted to see her hands resting there, bound by nothing more than his will, the picture of surrender.

Next time he had her in his bed, they were going to truly

indulge in bondage. He would tie her to his headboard and play with her for hours on end.

Then it occurred to Colm the loss of vision was yet another reason this all felt surreal, almost magical. He relied on his sense of sight as much as his ability to issue commands. Tonight was a challenge, and damn if he didn't love every second of it.

Sliding lower, he ran his tongue through the valley of her breasts, teased her belly button, then settled in right where he wanted to be, though her panties were still in the way.

She lifted her hips, clearly expecting him to help her take them off.

Nope. Not yet.

Her hips lowered when it became clear he wasn't going to strip them off her.

Colm ran his fingers over her silk-covered pussy, knowing his touch would be muted by her panties.

She shifted, trying to capture more. He wondered if he could make her break her vow of silence. If he could drive her so insane, she'd beg him to take her, scream out his name.

He liked the challenge of that, as well.

He rubbed his nose against her panties, breathing in the scent of her arousal. Her panties were damp, and she was so fucking *hot*.

God.

Once again, he had to find a way to steady himself, to regain control of his baser instincts, the ones telling him to rip off her damn panties and take her already.

Rising up until he was kneeling between her outstretched thighs, he pushed a finger beneath the elastic, seeking and finding her clit. He stroked it once, twice, three times, just light touches. Her hips undulated, her feet digging into the mattress to either side of him as she tried to lift herself toward his finger, needing more.

He touched her again, still keeping it light, gently caressing her until he heard her huff of impatience.

Colm breathed out a quiet laugh, then gave in, rubbing her more firmly, increasing the pace of his strokes as her hips rose and fell, adding her own pressure to the dance.

"Ah ah ah!" she breathed out, in rhythm with his fingers as he rubbed her clit, drawing out her arousal. His fingers dipped lower, gathering some of her wetness before he moved back to her clit, stroking her even faster now.

He wanted her to come this way the first time. Wanted to hear the sounds she made when she was close, when she went over. Without the benefit of his eyes or their words, he was forced to use his other senses, to become attuned to her sounds, the way her body moved, even the sweet scent of her arousal.

He wet his fingers again in her pussy, then returned to her clit. It only took a dozen more strokes before her body went stiff, her breathing stopped completely, and he felt her go over.

The orgasm escaped from her in one long, loud sigh, and she sank into his bed as if every bone in her body had melted.

He grinned, loving the way she softened, the tension that had been present in her just a few seconds earlier as she strove for the peak suddenly gone. Just like that. Vanished. In one stellar climax.

It was just the beginning.

Gripping the elastic of her panties, he slid them down her legs, tossing them over his shoulder to the bottom of the bed. Her legs parted in obvious invitation, and he felt her ankles against his lower back as she attempted to pull him toward her.

She was impatient, greedy, needy. Colm felt the same way.

Jesus. When was the last time he'd found a lover who was so compatible, so in tune with his own desires?

Too fucking long ago.

Maybe never.

Colm struggled to wrap his head around how different Brooke was in bed. He'd actually been considering whether or not he wanted to continue going out with her, but after tonight, there was no question the answer was hell yeah. He sure the fuck did.

He lowered his mouth to her pussy and ran his tongue along her slit as she gasped. She was still sensitive from her orgasm. Something he was more than happy to take advantage of.

Colm nipped at her clit, his hands holding her firmly to the mattress, despite her attempt to lift her hips toward him. He was running the show tonight.

A dominant lover, Colm wanted her submission as much as he wanted her out of her mind with desire.

He pushed his tongue inside her, fucking her with it as she thrashed beneath him. He waited for the begging, but apparently Brooke was made of stronger stuff.

Especially when he felt her hands return to his hair. She pulled it, roughly, intentionally, letting him know without words that she would only obey as long as it suited her.

God. She poked the bear...in all the best ways.

He sucked her clit into his mouth as he thrust three

fingers inside her hot, wet pussy, one hard shove that buried them deep. Her back arched in delight, then she took over, thrusting her hips up and down, driving his fingers in and out the way she wanted. Unable to keep his mouth on her, he used his thumb instead, rubbing her clit until she reached her climax again, keening quietly as she fell apart once more.

Colm pushed himself up, kneeling between her outstretched legs. He was just about to reach for the condom when she moved. One moment, she was lifeless on his bed, the next she was kneeling before him, her head dipping low as she took him into her mouth.

He grunted as her lips wrapped around the head of his cock, showing him no mercy as she sucked hard.

His hands flew to her hair, the tables turned as she drove him out of his mind. He gave her a taste of her own medicine, gripping and pulling her hair. Her groan against his cock told him just how much she loved it.

Fuck. They were made for each other.

Colm suffered only a second of regret that they weren't as compatible out of bed as they were in, but he didn't have time to worry about it for long, when Brooke took him deeper. Her fist gripped the base of his dick tightly—and she used that hold and her mouth to fuck him into oblivion.

He nearly let her drive him over the peak that way, but he didn't want to come in her mouth. He had to be inside her. *Now*.

He pushed her off his cock, cupped her face, and kissed her hard, with all the passion she inspired inside him. Their tongues fought for dominance as she gripped his hips, pulling him closer to her.

Colm broke the kiss after several long minutes. Reaching

for the nightstand, he fumbled around until he was able to grab one of the condoms he'd left there.

He felt her go still, her hand resting over his as if to stop him from donning the rubber.

He paused, curious.

Did she want to stop? There was no way he'd read her desire, her needs *that* wrong.

Had he?

Lifting her hand away, she reached down, gripping his cock once more, silently giving him the green light to continue.

He didn't move immediately, concerned about her hesitation. However, as she'd done several times tonight, his concerns vanished when she reached lower and gripped his balls, fondling them before moving her hand even farther back, the tip of one finger toying with his anus.

He sucked in a harsh breath as he gripped her wrists, chuckling under his breath. She was a wildcat—and he needed her.

Right. Fucking. Now.

Colm quickly slid the condom on, then pushed her to her back. He placed the head of his cock at her opening, pausing for just a moment as he recalled her hand halting him from putting on the condom.

He wanted to give her one last chance to stop him if this wasn't truly what she wanted.

She did the opposite. Instead, she tilted her hips, wrapped her ankles around his waist, and pulled him inside.

Colm was helpless to resist. He thrust into her in one hard, fast motion, loving her breathy gasp and the tight clench of her inner muscles against him.

After that, all semblance of control, any tentative grip of restraint he might have held on to, disappeared as he took her like a man possessed.

She met him hard thrust for hard thrust, lifting up to meet him, urging him on as her fingernails scored his back and her harsh groans begged for more.

Colm could have come way too fast. God knew he wanted to, but dammit...he wanted more.

He pulled out and she reached for him, huffing out an angry breath.

Until he grasped her hips and flipped her over. She quickly went up on her hands and knees in front of him, the two of them losing no time reconnecting.

Colm slammed in roughly and she was right there, pressing back against him, forcing him to take her faster.

He gripped her hips, using that hold to move her with even more power. At this rate, they were bound to break each other. And yet, it still didn't feel like enough.

He knew her climax sounds now, could tell from her breathing she was close.

Fuck. He was too.

Reaching out, he found her hair. Using a firm grip, he guided her upper body toward him, wrapping his free arm around her so he could touch her breast, squeezing it, pinching her nipple. The two of them continued moving into each other, closer—so fucking close—to the brink.

Releasing her hair, he shifted his fingers lower, stroking her clit. Just a half dozen rough touches and it was over. For her *and* for him.

Her pussy muscles contracted, squeezing his cock so hard, he saw stars as he came. He grunted loudly as she—

once again—fell silently, with a hard jerk that had her body going stiff before the air seeped out of her in one long exhale.

He could get addicted to that response. That sound. Big time.

She was the first to move, falling forward, facedown. Her breathing growing softer, slower.

She was asleep within seconds.

He chuckled quietly, tugged off the condom, tossing it toward where he thought his trash can was, then he followed her down, spooning her from behind, feeling like a teenage boy with his first girlfriend, almost fucking giddy.

She was perfect for him.

In bed.

If only he felt this happy with her outside of the bedroom.

CHAPTER FIVE

K elli awoke with a start, confused. The room was
pitch-black, which was weird. Her bedroom was
never this dark. The streetlights outside always
ensured she could see around the room.

An arm around her waist shifted as a hand snaked up to
cup her breast—and suddenly she remembered.

The party. The blackout. The game.

She'd passed out in Colm's room after too much wine,
finished partying for the night. What she hadn't counted on
was Robbie crawling into bed with her.

She vaguely recalled him waking her up, whispering to
ask if they were doing this. She'd been too confused to
respond, and then too late to ask what he meant because he'd
started kissing her.

Kelli hadn't recalled Robbie's kisses being so...God...so
fucking hot. The two of them hadn't slept together in college.
They'd really only gone out on a handful of dates, until one
night, they'd both admitted they were better off as friends.

While she found Robbie physically attractive—then and now —she hadn't felt any sexual attraction toward him, and he'd confessed the same.

Colm claimed her type of guy was one she could control. That she wanted relationships where she called the shots. But he'd been wrong. He'd mistaken what she wanted with what she'd always, unfortunately, found—weak-willed guys who were all too happy to follow her lead. It was why she'd always walked away...bored and frustrated.

None of that had been present in Robbie tonight. When their three-decades-long kiss ended earlier, she'd started to ask him what the hell he was doing.

But he'd floored her when he'd placed his fingers on her lips and shushed her. It was a tiny gesture that had packed a wallop for some reason. Perhaps because it had felt like a command rather than a request.

And she'd consumed just enough wine and vodka and tequila—and suffered far too many lonely nights lately—to resist it.

She and Robbie hadn't really discussed the hows of his sperm donation, though the man was a science teacher, for God's sake, so she figured he had to know it wouldn't involve sex. But...she hadn't spelled that out either. In her defense, he'd only just said yes at dinner, and they'd agreed to wait until the Christmas break to—Jesus—*transfer the funds*.

Thanks so much for that description, Colm.

Anyway, Robbie had said yes, and that was where the conversation had ended.

If she'd had a clearer head—and more time—she probably would have called a halt to tonight's sexcapade, but Robbie kept distracting her with amazing kisses and—holy crap—the guy had managed to find approximately fifty-nine erogenous zones on her body she didn't even know about. After that, she didn't give a damn about anything other than coming.

She must have fallen asleep after the last earth-shattering orgasm, though she didn't have a clue how long she'd been out.

Robbie placed another soft kiss on her shoulder, and she opened her mouth, about to ask if he was ready for round two.

She didn't say it though. They'd spent the entire evening in this bed, blind and mute, and fuck if it didn't turn her on. She wasn't ready to end that game. There would be plenty of time to talk this out tomorrow.

Given his heavy, slow breathing and his gentle, almost lethargic touches, she wondered if he was fully awake. She sighed, blissfully, loving the feeling of his arms around her. The tenderness, the comfort of it, was something she hadn't experienced in a very long time. She slowly wiggled her ass against him, suddenly aware that he was hard and ready to go.

He nuzzled against her, his nose in her hair as he pressed more sweet kisses to the back of her head, and his arm tightened. She reached around until she found his ass, feeling the need to do a little exploring herself. The first time, the pleasure—times three—had been all hers. She couldn't remember the last time she'd been with such a patient, attentive lover who knew exactly what the fuck he was doing.

Then she realized why she couldn't remember.

It had never happened.

She started to roll over, but he stopped her, tightened his

grip in this sexy spoon. Kelli tried again—shocked when Robbie lifted his hand and slapped her ass. Just once, but it wasn't a tap. It actually stung.

Once more, Kelli tried to make this guy fit with what she'd always believed about Robbie. She came up short.

More than that, she was starting to wonder if she'd missed the boat back in college.

She tried to twist again, ready to see just how alpha he was.

Kelli wasn't disappointed when she heard his dark, deep chuckle and felt him shift on the bed. He pulled her to her hands and knees, one firm hand flat on her stomach, the other stroking her ass.

"Ahh," she gasped when he spanked her again.

This time, he didn't hold back, and he continued to pepper her ass with stinging slaps that hurt...in a surprisingly hot way.

Kelli opened her mouth to...what? Tell him to stop? Beg him for more?

It was too much, too good. And she was afraid if she spoke, the spell would be broken. He would stop.

She lowered her upper body, shifting from her hands to her elbows, keeping her ass lifted high. She wasn't sure how she could tell her actions had pleased him, but there was a definite shift in him, in the way he gently caressed her sore ass that told her he approved.

The whole night had been spent issuing unspoken demands and pleas, speaking only through body language, sighs and moans.

Like right now.

Kelli sighed when he ran his fingers along her slit, slipping two inside her. She arched her back, pushing toward them, wanting—*needing* more.

He didn't disappoint as he stroked her harder, faster.

God, she'd never had a lover work so hard to make sure she found her pleasure, and there was something about the way he was touching her right now that told her he wasn't going to stop until she came.

His fingers left her, and she growled. The sound clearly amused him as he gave a breathy laugh—all air, no sound.

And then he repeated the whole thing again. Spanking her, rubbing her heated skin, fucking her with those two fingers.

Over and over, until finally, he added a third finger to the game.

Kelli was lost, especially when the hand on her stomach slipped lower and he stroked her clit.

Her body reacted before her brain could catch up, lightning tingling from her pussy, pulsating up her spine. She gasped and groaned, the sounds muted by the pillow beneath her.

He gave her no time to recover. Instead, he donned a condom, pushing into her still-quivering pussy, straight to the hilt.

She had only a split second to wonder about the condom—it was the second time he'd used one—before he took her with all the speed and force she'd ever dreamed of.

His fingers clenched tightly into her hips as he pulled her toward him on every inward thrust.

Kelli realized she wasn't an active participant at the moment. She hadn't found her sea legs yet, still reeling from the first orgasm.

Not that he cared. He wanted her. So he took her.

It was heady, passionate, everything she'd ever dreamed about but never found.

Her second climax struck fast and hard, her body trembling as if she'd received one hell of an electric shock. He didn't acknowledge it, didn't slow down.

"Ahh!" she yelled into the pillow, uncertain she could withstand another orgasm like that. Even as her traitorous hips began pushing back toward him, demanding that he take her harder.

Every thrust felt like flint against steel, sparking hotter, making her burn.

Then his thumb found its way to her ass, the tip rubbing around the entrance.

Oh my God.

He wiggled it suggestively—that was it, just a suggestion —and she was lost. When she came again, she took him down with her. Both of them jerking against each other, taking as much as they could, roughly, gracelessly.

Kelli's knees gave out, sliding down until she lay prostrate on the bed, facedown.

Robbie turned as he fell to his back next to her, his hand resting on the heated flesh of her ass.

She huffed out a laugh when he lifted it lazily, placing one last smack there, before she heard his breath deepen, sleep taking him.

Kelli was only a moment behind him, her eyes drifting shut. Her last cognizant thought was that she'd never felt so... content, sated.

Happy.

. . .

THE NEXT TIME Kelli opened her eyes, the darkness that had permeated the room had brightened to a dark slate gray. It was still hard to see, but Kelli knew morning had arrived. She shifted slowly, grinning at the stiffness in muscles that hadn't gotten that good of a workout in way too long. She'd passed out on the edge of the bed, so it was very easy for her to sit up without jarring Robbie, who was still sound asleep.

She sighed, blissfully, blinking to try to bring some part of the room into focus. Colm was going to kill her when she confessed to having sex in his bed.

Not that the thought dimmed her smile. It actually only made the whole night that much better.

Her head hurt, but not as badly as she might have expected. And she was thirsty, her mouth bone-dry. Neither of those things bothered her as much as they might have if last night hadn't been so...perfect.

She rose gingerly, secretly loving the soreness between her legs.

She'd missed sex, even the lackluster variety she'd endured the past few years.

Now...God...

Kelli wasn't certain she'd be able to settle for anything less than what she and Robbie had shared last night.

Robbie.

She turned to look at him, but he faced away from her. She admired his bare, muscular back. She hadn't realized he was so strong, so physically built. He hid way too much of the good stuff under his loose-fitting T-shirts.

Glancing around the room, she spotted her Merida dress laying in a heap near the corner. She hadn't thought to bring a change of clothes, which was stupid. She'd known she was spending the night, but she'd been running late and figured she'd just borrow something from Darcy for the return trip home.

She stood up and stretched. The shifting of the mattress didn't wake Robbie, but it roused him enough that he turned over, his arm claiming the spot she'd just vacated.

Kelli started to bend down to see if she could wake him with a kiss, but as she shifted closer...

Fuck.

No.

Fuck no.

She backed away from the bed quickly, her heart suddenly lodged in her throat, her lungs constricted so tightly, she couldn't breathe.

Padraig?

She shook her head, sheer panic clawing at her, as she studied the sleeping form on the bed in the dimly lit room.

Not Robbie.

Padraig's clean-shaven face was peaceful as he slept.

Kelli's brain was on system overload as she tried to figure out what was going on.

Padraig had been drunk last night. *Very* drunk. And sad about Mia and upset about almost losing Seamus.

Had he sought her out? For sex?

No.

Jesus, no. He wouldn't do that. It didn't make sense.

He shifted again and she reacted before she could think.

Escape.

The headache she'd thought bearable was now a blinding migraine, and she suddenly felt nauseous.

She had to get the fuck out of there.

Kelli quickly reached for her dress, shoving it on, only bothering to zip it halfway up her back.

Where the fuck are my shoes?

Downstairs. The rest of her stuff was downstairs.

Tiptoeing to the door, she left the room, managing to get her stuff and get out of the apartment—and closed pub—without running into anyone.

Dashing across the street in her ridiculous ballgown—talk about the ultimate Halloween walk of shame—she got into her car and stared out the windshield without seeing anything around her. Her hands were trembling as one thought kept beating a tempo in her aching head.

What the hell have I done?

CHAPTER SIX

Kelli stood outside Pat's Pub a week later and cursed herself for being such a damn coward. Running away last Saturday had been wrong. Stupid.

But she'd been hungover, shocked, and God...so freaked out.

So she'd gone home, taken some Advil, crawled into her own bed, and slept until dinnertime. After that, she'd gone on autopilot, sleepwalking through her days, tossing and turning all night.

At work, she was able to forget what they'd done before coming home and staring at her phone for hours, wondering and worrying what it meant that Padraig hadn't called or texted her.

Then chastising herself for not calling or texting *him*.

On Wednesday, Padraig put her out of her misery.

Sort of.

He'd texted to see if she'd recovered from the party. She'd responded with one tentative word.

Yes.

Just yes.

Then he'd given her a "me too—barely," followed by LOL and "See you Friday?"

And that was it.

Again, she'd just said yes, assuming he wanted to talk about what had happened after the party face-to-face. It was just like Padraig. He was sensible and kind and not a complete chicken shit, like her. Obviously, he wasn't angry at her for leaving or upset about what had happened. She could have saved herself a lot of angst if she'd just stuck around the morning after. They could have talked it out, laughed it off, and moved on.

Except...Kelli wasn't sure she could do any of those things.

She wanted to. Desperately. But...he'd rocked her world. Shaken her to the core. Good sex was pretty rare in her realm of experience.

Great, amazing sex? Unheard of.

Plus, Padraig had been her best friend since kindergarten, and never, not once in all those years, had she looked at him as anything more than the brother she'd never had.

Now...she kept remembering Friday night. The way he'd kissed her, spanked her, held her. It was fucking hot.

But even now, a week out, she couldn't make the pieces fit. Because Padraig still loved Mia, deeply. He hadn't gotten over her death and he wasn't ready to move on.

She knew that because she was his best friend, and in a

lot of ways, she felt like she knew him better than she knew herself.

So. No.

Nothing fit here.

She glanced through the plate-glass window and spotted Padraig behind the bar, pouring drinks, talking and laughing with Emmy.

He looked and acted exactly the same.

Meanwhile, she felt as if she was someone completely different, a stranger to herself.

She'd been doing Friday happy hours at the pub for years, but this week...God, this week it was taking everything she had to walk into the place.

"This is Paddy," she murmured, trying to reassure herself that they could talk this out, make things right.

She couldn't lose him over this. She wouldn't.

Steeling herself, she opened the door and walked in, walked right over to the counter and claimed her stool.

Padraig gave her the same sweet, friendly smile he always gave her, the one reserved just for her, and she felt like she could breathe for the first time in days.

"There's Merida! How was your week, Kell?" he asked.

She glanced from Padraig to Emmy, then back again. He was acting like, well, like Padraig.

So she gave him the same. "A whole week of five-year-olds hopped up on Halloween candy. I'll let you puzzle out the answer to that."

He laughed and lifted a wine bottle.

She raised her hand with an unspoken "stop" cue. "God, no."

Padraig laughed harder. "Yeah. I hear you. Pretty sure

it's going to be a damn long time before I drink again. Maybe years. Maybe never. I'm a little embarrassed." He glanced at Emmy. "Okay, I'm a lot embarrassed."

Emmy giggled. "I didn't say a word."

"So...it was a rough Saturday?" Kelli asked, trying to figure out how to start the conversation they needed to have. Unfortunately, the pub was quite busy, and it would be tough to pull him aside for a few minutes. She also really didn't want to talk this out with Emmy there.

That had been another layer to this week's unending guilt. The fact that Kelli genuinely believed Emmy and Padraig would make a wonderful couple, that she could be the woman to heal her best friend's shattered heart.

He nodded. "Oh yeah."

"Rough Friday night too," Emmy added with a laugh.

Kelli was taken aback. Had Padraig confided what happened to Emmy? "Was it?" she asked, looking at him.

"I blacked out, Kell. I've never done that in my life, and I'm ashamed to admit it now, but I don't remember the end of that party *at all*. I'm not sure how I let myself go that far."

Kelli could suddenly hear her pulse thudding in her ears, her heart beating so fast, so hard, so fucking loud.

Emmy and Padraig said something, the two of them laughing, but Kelli couldn't hear them over her own panic.

He didn't remember. He didn't know what they'd done.

"Pour me a pint of Guinness, Paddy, and keep 'em coming."

Kelli glanced over as Colm claimed the spot next to her. He looked as bad as she felt. His dark hair was mussed, like he'd run his hand through it a hundred times too many, and he had dark circles under his eyes. Plus, he'd gotten a little heavy-handed with the trimmers, his beard shorter than normal, even a bit patchy in places.

He looked like shit.

"You okay?" she asked, despite the fact she was in freak-out mode.

A-fucking-gain.

Padraig didn't remember having sex with her. What the fuck was she supposed to do now?

Colm shrugged. His response little more than a grunt. "Yeah."

"Still not returning your calls?" Padraig asked, as Kelli forced herself to listen to their conversation, needing the distraction.

"Who?" she asked.

"Brooke." Colm didn't bother to elaborate.

"Apparently, she and my brother here had one hell of an after-party the night of Halloween." Padraig looked ready to continue the tale, but someone at a nearby table called his name, asking for another round. "I'll be right back."

"Do you mind watching my laptop real quick?" Emmy asked, excusing herself to go to the ladies' room.

Kelli waved her assent. "So you hit a homer, huh?" she asked, confused by his misery.

Colm nodded. "Best sex I've had in a long time. Maybe ever."

Kelli could relate to that. She felt the same way about her night with Padraig. And he couldn't even remember it. "Wow. Didn't realize Regina George had it in her," she said, working hard to adopt the teasing tone reserved pretty much exclusively for Colm.

"Neither did I. In fact, I was debating breaking things off with her."

"After you had sex with her, of course."

Despite the fact he looked like he'd been ridden hard and put up wet, Colm managed to give her his signature cocky grin. "Of course after. Jesus. I'm not an idiot."

"And now she's not returning your calls?" Kelli asked. Then, without waiting for an answer, she added, "Good for her. Starting to respect Brooke more."

Colm ignored her. "No. She's not returning my calls. Or my texts. I'm starting to feel like a creepy stalker. I just can't figure out..."

"Have you considered that maybe it wasn't as great for *her*?"

Colm smirked. "That thought never crossed my mind. Because I know it was. That many orgasms don't lie."

"You realize women can fake those, right?"

Colm took a long swig of his beer. "Nope. Not fake. I'd know."

"Says every man on the planet. Yet most women *are* faking them. That's pretty simple math."

"No. It was good for her too. I know it was. Which is why I can't... Aw, fuck it. I'm tired of talking about it. Tired of thinking about it." Colm set his pint glass down and stroked his beard before running his hand through his hair.

"You're going to go bald if you keep tugging at it like that," she said.

And then, she recalled her conversation with Colm last week, the way he'd really listened and been supportive of her decision to have a baby on her own.

Padraig was gathering up empty glasses from a table nearby, and Emmy was on her way back from the bathroom.

"Can I talk to you, Colm?" she asked. "In private."

He looked somewhat surprised by the request, but he recovered quickly. "Sure." He picked up his beer glass and headed to a table near the bar.

"No," she said, stopping him with a hand on his forearm. "Over there." She pointed to a booth in the far corner. She couldn't risk anyone overhearing what she was going to say.

Colm gestured for her to lead the way.

Once they were settled in the booth, he said, "What's up? Something go wrong with the sperm donor?"

She shook her head, not surprised he assumed that was what she wanted to talk about. Right now, he and Robbie were the only two people who knew about her plans to have a baby.

"No. It's about Halloween. I..." She swallowed heavily, her mouth suddenly going dry.

She reached across the table and grabbed Colm's Guinness, taking a long swig as his eyebrows rose.

"What about it?"

"I, um...well, I... Fuck. I slept with Paddy."

Colm tilted his head, and for a moment, she could almost imagine him trying to figure out if he'd heard her correctly. "Slept with or had sex with?"

"Sex," she whispered.

Colm shook his head. "That's not possible. Paddy hasn't said a word to me about—"

"He was blacked out. Doesn't remember."

"I'm pretty fucking sure he'd remember that, Kell."

"He doesn't, okay?" She hadn't meant to raise her voice,

but she was running on fumes at the moment, her nerves stretched taut.

"Okay. You're going to have to work with me here though. I mean...even if he doesn't remember, *you* weren't that drunk. Why would you—"

"It was dark—pitch-black. I thought he was Robbie."

Colm chuckled. "Jesus. Only you could manage to sleep with the wrong guy."

"Oh my God, you're an asshole."

"Wait," Colm said, raising his hand to ward off her fury. "You thought you were sleeping with the sperm donor, but it was really Paddy?"

"Yeah. And now I don't know what the hell to do."

"What do you mean? Do about what?"

"About telling him! I mean, I slept with my *best friend*, who is still reeling from losing his wife. It's going to crush him when I tell him! He'll feel like he wasn't loyal to Mia's memory, and he'll..." She sucked in a deep breath, unable to finish her thought.

Colm fell silent, and she took comfort in the fact he was genuinely thinking it through, trying to find a way to help her. She followed his gaze, the two of them glancing back at Padraig who was mixing up a batch of margaritas.

She and Colm were probably the only two people—with the exception of Pop Pop—who recognized the subtle differences in Padraig since Mia's death. The lines by his eyes that hadn't been there before he'd walked every step of the way through her illness beside her, the tightness around his mouth, the way his smile never seemed to fill his entire face the way it had when they were all younger. He moved just a little bit slower, held himself just a little bit stiffer.

It seemed like every second of every day, he was fighting just to remain upright. It had been two years, but Kelli knew Padraig's heart ached for Mia just as much now as it had the day she'd died.

"I think you should wait to tell him," Colm said at last.

"How long?"

He shrugged. "At least through the holidays. And maybe even longer. Maybe never. I think what we have to decide is what purpose would telling him serve."

Kelli liked the way Colm said "we." It helped that she wasn't alone in this. "No purpose. It would hurt him."

Colm nodded. "Yeah, but...well...would it hurt *you* not to tell him?"

Kelli wasn't sure how to respond to that. Did she admit to Colm how much that night in Padraig's arms had affected her, made her long for things she thought she'd managed to convince herself she didn't need?

"That night...it was...he was... I've never experienced anything like that. It was incredible." She lifted her shoulder casually as if that would downplay her confession. It didn't.

Colm reached across the table and squeezed her hand. "Are you sure you haven't given up on the possibility of finding love?"

"I haven't. I told you—wanting a baby and finding love don't have to go hand in hand. Besides, if I've learned anything from Halloween, it's that I'm an even bigger dumpster fire than I thought."

Colm smirked. "I could have told you that." She narrowed her eyes, but before she could call him to task, he sobered up and said, "I'm sorry, Kell."

Kelli swallowed, trying to dislodge the lump in her

throat. Then she fought to force a smile. "It's okay. He's my best friend, and I can't...I *won't* do anything to jeopardize that. I can take this secret to the grave."

"Can you?"

She nodded. She could. She really could. "Ignorance is bliss."

She wasn't sure where those words came from, but the tone definitely didn't match the phrase. Because she wasn't sure whose ignorance she was referring to.

Hers or Padraig's.

Wasn't it better that Padraig not know he'd betrayed Mia's memory? Because that was how he would view what they'd done.

And wasn't it now worse for her because she'd had a glimpse of something she feared she would never have, never feel, again? What would she give to have that ignorance back again?

"Yeah. It is." The way Colm looked at her, the tone of his voice drove home the feeling she'd had last week. That she and Colm had more in common than they'd realized.

"So...Brooke," she prompted, realizing she'd brushed him off at the bar, making jokes, while he'd tried to help her.

A sadness she'd rarely seen crept into his eyes. "I felt something that night, Kell. Something I...really haven't felt before. I actually thought she might be the one."

"Wow," she said, fighting to lighten the heaviness surrounding them. "That girl must have a magic va-jay-jay if she's got you thinking commitment. You realize you're still six years away from the 'not marrying before forty' deadline."

She expected him to laugh, but instead, he just agreed. "I

know. It knocked me on my ass because there was a connection there. And I liked it. I *really* fucking liked it."

Kelli nodded because she got it. She glanced at Padraig once more, still struggling to assimilate her best friend with the lover who'd rocked her world. "You liked it so much it actually had you thinking marriage?"

Colm blew out a long breath. "I don't know. That night felt different from everything that had come before with her. I really wanted to see her again, talk to her, try to figure out if what happened between us... God. She's like two different women. Outside the bedroom, she talks a lot... about nothing. But when we were in bed together, it felt like she was made for me. I'm having a hard time making the pieces fit."

Jesus. Kelli wasn't sure how to reply to that—because she'd had the same problem this week. Exactly the same problem.

"Not that it matters now. She's completely stonewalling me. So..."

"So, what's the answer here?" she asked.

"Karaoke," Colm said.

She frowned. "I've spent way too many years surrounded by the Collins family because I sadly understand that response."

"We're doing it here in the pub. Next Thursday night. You and me are going to get drunk and sing our blues away."

She raised her hand, shaking her head. "Nope. No alcohol. I've given it up. Forever."

Colm glanced at his beer, and she recalled the big swig she'd just taken.

"Starting now," she said with a smirk.

"Excellent." Colm lifted his phone and immediately started texting.

"What are you doing? And what's excellent?"

"Group text with my cousins. I'm starting up the annual 'Kelli's on the wagon again' pool. Gonna start the wagering on how long it'll last this time."

She shot him an eat-shit-and-die scowl. "You're a dick."

"Hey, Colm," Padraig yelled across the bar, holding up his cell phone. "Put me down for ten bucks. I say she caves on Friendsgiving."

"*Et tu*, Paddy?" Kelli yelled, her heart fluttering when he laughed at her joke, but she wasn't sure if her response was driven by relief or disappointment.

She caught Colm looking at her, and she was touched by the concern she saw there.

"I'm fine," she murmured.

He gave her a friendly wink. "Yeah. Me too. Face it. The two of us should be used to this crap by now."

Kelli laughed. "Right? You keep talking about the Collins curse, but damn if I wouldn't love to be struck down by that thing. I feel like I'm standing right under it with my arms out, screaming 'come on, hit me with your best shot.' Aaaand nothing."

"So the other night didn't change your mind about going the single-mom route?"

"Nope. It convinced me even more I've made the right decision. I can't even manage to get drunken one-night stands right. I'm better off taking a break from men for a while. Focus on what will make me happy. And for me, that's a baby. Are you really reconsidering your bachelor status?"

Colm didn't reply right away, and when he did, she couldn't help but think that he was lying. "Not a bit."

"So, we forge on."

"Yeah."

Neither of them sounded particularly happy about that, but what else could they do? "Well," she glanced at her phone, "happy hour is clearly over. This place is starting to get crowded with the Friday night regulars, and since I'm not really in a party mood..."

Colm nodded. "Me either. What are you doing tonight?"

She shrugged. "I'll probably just go home, find an old movie on Netflix, and chill out."

"Yeah. That's my plan too. Wanna do that together?"

She grinned. "Seriously? Is this going to start becoming a thing? You and me hanging out together?"

He narrowed his eyes. "It's just a damn movie, Kell. And I'm tired of watching them by myself."

"Ditto."

Then he gave her a wicked grin. "Even so, don't go setting your heart on winning mine. You might be taking yourself off the market for a little while, but this rolling stone still has a lot of miles to go. You coming?"

She rolled her eyes and pretended to gag at the thought of them together.

Then she followed him upstairs.

CHAPTER SEVEN

C olm sat at the bar next to Pop Pop, the two of them enjoying—well, currently tolerating—the karaoke performances. Right now, there was a married couple onstage butchering "Love Shack."

"You giving us a song tonight, lad?" Pop Pop asked. "Always enjoyed listening to you sing."

Colm nodded. "Yeah. Kelli and I already signed up. We're doing a duet."

Padraig, who was standing across the counter from them, filling a pitcher from the tap, paused. "You and Kelli? *My* Kelli?"

Colm wasn't sure why it tweaked his nerves to hear Padraig refer to Kelli as his. They'd all grown up together, all been friends since practically the cradle, so was the possessive adjective really necessary?

He pushed that annoyance aside. Padraig's comment would have been perfectly valid two weeks ago.

However, something had changed between him and

Kelli since she'd revealed her plan to become a mother to him.

Last Friday, he'd felt pretty damn low, depressed and confused by Brooke's sudden silent treatment. Kelli—of all people—had managed to cheer him up and actually make him feel better. They'd watched a couple Will Ferrell movies, pigged out on popcorn, and at the end of the night, he'd hugged her goodbye when she left. The gesture had felt surprisingly...normal. Natural.

Right.

Shit.

He wasn't sure what was going on, but she'd returned Sunday to watch the football games, just like she always did. The two of them had sat next to each other, cheering for the Ravens with the rest of his family, but every time her leg accidentally brushed his, he sort of...felt something.

Something he didn't dare put a name to.

And unbeknownst to Padraig—to everyone—the two of them had started having dinner together this week.

Three dinners in a row—twice at restaurants, and then last night at her place—where they'd talked about everything under the sun.

He and Kelli spoke the same language—sarcasm—and he'd finally admitted his mother hadn't been wrong when she said he and Kelli were similar souls. They'd found they had a lot of things in common, so conversation between them flowed easily, equal measures insightful and funny as shit.

So now, when Padraig stood here and called her "his Kelli," it bothered Colm. More than he cared to admit. Because she was his friend too.

"What song are you going to sing for us?" Pop Pop asked.

Colm grinned because he knew his grandfather was going to love his answer. "Jackson."

Just as he expected, Pop Pop's eyes widened. "You know I'm a sucker for a Johnny and June song, lad."

"Kelli picked it out. And I'm sure it was for you."

He, Padraig, and Kelli had all been members of chorus in high school, even participating in the school musicals, so it wasn't like the two of them hadn't sung together before. They just hadn't sung together in a long time...or without a big group of people around them.

"Speak of the devil," Pop Pop said as Kelli walked up to them. She gave his grandfather a quick kiss on the cheek.

"How's my boyfriend?" she asked. She and Pop Pop had been pretending to be boyfriend and girlfriend for years.

"Colm tells me you're singing one of my favorites tonight. You know how I love your voice, dear lass."

Kelli was a hell of a singer, with a powerful, soulful mezzo-soprano voice. Pop Pop swore she'd missed her calling, that she could have been as famous as Aunt Teagan if she'd put her mind to it. Kelli always blushed and dismissed the compliment as just that—kind words from a beloved old man.

"You *have* to say that," she teased. "I'm your girlfriend."

Pop Pop chuckled. "You remind me so much of my sweet Sunday."

Colm had never heard him say that, but given Kelli's response, it appeared the comment wasn't a new one.

"You and Paddy are both clearly blind. No one except the two of you ever calls me sweet."

"You're sweet, Kell," Colm said, the words falling out before he could think better of them.

Padraig and Pop Pop both looked at him, Padraig with shock...and Pop Pop with something much more dangerous—a knowing amusement that seemed to scream "Gotcha!"

Kelli was oblivious to the undercurrents because she just rolled her eyes and scoffed. "Sure I am. I'm a regular bundle of cotton candy. I just came over to let you know we're next up, Colm. Hope your fragile ego is going to be okay with me stealing the spotlight, Johnny."

He chuckled. "Dream on, June. I think we both know who's going to carry this number. Just try to keep up. And don't embarrass me. I have a karaoke reputation to uphold."

"Phew," Padraig said. "There we go. I was starting to worry about you two."

Colm rose from the stool, happy to step away from the quiet scrutiny of his grandfather, who was still looking from Colm to Kelli and back again. Not that Colm expected to be let off the hook completely. Pop Pop was definitely going to question him later.

He only hoped he had an answer by the time he did.

The couple onstage had just finished scream-singing "Love Shack" as he and Kelli approached. Uncle Sean, who was serving as the karaoke deejay tonight, gave them both a wink as he introduced them. As they stepped onstage, they adjusted the microphone stands to their heights—which in their cases meant raising both of them.

Kelli stepped over and gave him a quick hip check and a grin as the music started. He rolled his eyes, then leaned in, the two of them doing their best Johnny and June impersonations. Colm had a naturally deep voice, so channeling the man in black wasn't hard at all.

Kelli moved in time with the fast pace, laughing and

adopting June's attitude as well as sound. On the chorus, she stepped over, sharing his microphone, and the crowd cheered even louder than they already had been.

Their faces were close...and Colm felt the oddest desire to close the distance between them, to press his lips against hers.

He stumbled over a couple of words.

Shaking himself, he forced his eyes away from her face and back to the monitor flashing the lyrics, even though he knew all the words by heart.

Neither of them were strangers in the pub when it came to karaoke night, but they'd never sung together. He typically pulled out an Ed Sheeran song, while Kelli was partial to the ladies of the sixties—rocking out to Janis Joplin or Joni Mitchell. Colm suspected they were going to start getting countless requests for duets after this.

As the song ended, the audience gave them a standing ovation, the first of the night. He grasped her hand to steady her as they started to leave the stage, high-fiving Sean with the other. She started to pull her hand away once they'd taken the one step down to the floor, but he held firm, using it to tug her closer.

"You did okay," he said, acting as if her performance was subpar.

She leaned toward him, her breasts brushing against his arm.

Colm was surprised by the way his body reacted when her narrowed eyes. Jesus. His cock actually twitched and started to thicken.

Since when was that look a turn-on?

What the fuck was that about?

He released her hand.

"Oh, honey, I know you tried, but..." she said, lightly tapping his cheek. He suspected she was going to say more, to pile on her own playful insult, but something behind Colm caught her eye. "Shit. Incoming," she murmured.

Colm turned, taking a second to find what had captured her attention. Then he saw her—Brooke. Standing at a nearby table, looking at him.

When she caught his eye, she lifted her hand and waved, giving him a slightly nervous smile that told him she at least had the good grace to feel bad about leaving him high and dry the morning after. She had even left her panties—he'd found them in his bed the next day. They were currently on top of his dresser, sitting there like some goddamn souvenir, taunting him.

Kelli gave him a slight nudge. "Go talk to her. See if..."

She didn't finish her sentence, didn't have to. Kelli knew exactly how much that night with Brooke had rattled him, shaken up his well-ordered, no-rush-to-the-altar lifestyle.

He nodded, then gave Kelli a smile, feeling slightly torn. He'd been having a good time with her. So much so, he'd been able to push Brooke from his mind.

He no longer considered her his frenemy, but did he really think of her as a friend?

As *just* a friend?

Kelli leaned closer, her breath hot on his cheek, and once again he was overwhelmed by the desire to turn his head the slightest bit to kiss her.

"What are you waiting for?" she murmured, obviously confused by his hesitance, considering how many times he'd mentioned wondering why Brooke had vanished without a word.

"I...don't know."

She laughed quietly. "You're a lunatic, Colm. Go talk to the woman, you big chicken shit."

She'd referred to herself as that very same thing several times the past couple weeks, in regard to the way she'd turned tail and run rather than talking to Padraig. Although, neither of them was sure that was actually a bad thing.

Of course, her taunt struck a nerve, just like it always did. Only this time, he didn't feel the need to one-up her insult.

No. This time, he felt the need to drag her upstairs, pull her over his knee and spank her until she came.

Fuck.

His cock was now on full alert.

This wasn't good.

This was very, very bad.

When he still didn't move, Kelli tilted her head. "Are you okay?"

He nodded slowly, realizing he must *look* like a lunatic.

He wanted Kelli. He *really* wanted her.

Before he could think about that—Jesus, it would take a long time for that to soak in—he needed to talk to Brooke. He'd spent every night since Halloween, reliving every moment of their time in bed together. He'd jacked off to the memory more times than he could count...but he'd noticed the last few nights it had been Kelli's face he saw when he closed his eyes, instead of Brooke's.

Right now, he was torn and confused as fuck.

He turned away from Kelli and walked across the room. "Hi, Brooke."

She lifted her hand. "Hey, Colm. I was wondering if you had a minute? I wanted to talk to you."

He nodded. "Sure." Glancing around, he found an empty table toward the front of the pub, away from the singing and dancing and revelry around the stage. "Might be quieter up there."

The two of them walked to the table, sitting down. "Want a drink?" he asked, looking around for Padraig.

Brooke shook her head. "No. I can't stay long. I just wanted to apologize for Halloween."

"You left without saying goodbye," he said, fighting to keep his voice impassive. He and Brooke hadn't been in a relationship, hadn't made any commitments to each other. At least not with words. But damn if that night in his bed hadn't felt like...something that felt meaningful, important.

"I know. I shouldn't have done that. I'm afraid I had way too many screwdrivers. Between that and the blackout, I was a bit fuzzy when Robbie came in and we started making out."

Colm frowned. "What?"

"Well, I'm embarrassed to admit when Robbie came in, I thought it was you for a minute or two. I'd been waiting for you, so needless to say, it took him by surprise when I wrapped my arms around his neck and started kissing him."

"You and Robbie?" Colm knew Brooke had been tipsy that night, but he hadn't thought her so drunk she didn't even realize she'd been with him.

"Robbie thanked me for it when we broke apart, said it

was a great kiss. We both laughed. Obviously, I'd gone to the wrong bedroom. The thing is...it really *had* been a great kiss."

"You were in the wrong bedroom?" Colm realized he was parroting everything she said, but his brain was struggling to keep up.

If Brooke had been with Robbie that night, who the fuck had he...

His gaze traveled across the pub to where Kelli was sitting with Darcy and Sunnie, laughing.

His attention returned to Brooke, when he realized she was still talking.

"Anyway," Brooke said, still rambling on. "We started talking, and then, well, he kissed me again, and..."

"You left with Robbie."

She nodded, biting her lower lip, clearly feeling guilty. Colm had noticed Robbie and Brooke had hit it off at the party. The science teacher didn't seem to mind Brooke's never-ending talking.

"We've been going out since then. I'm so sorry I avoided your calls and texts. I just didn't know how to tell you. And that was wrong. I really am sorry."

"It's okay, Brooke. Honest. I'm happy for you and Robbie."

She blushed. "Thanks. I know it's early, but God, I kind of think he might be the one."

Colm smiled. Brooke and Robbie had been in the Collins Dorm just one time, and they'd both been struck down by the curse. "That's great."

"Well. Um. He's actually waiting for me in the parking lot. We have dinner plans tonight. He wanted to come in himself to apologize, but I asked to do it alone."

"You and I weren't in a relationship, Brooke."

"I know," she said quickly. "But that night..." She lifted one shoulder. "I was wrong to leave with him, without telling you."

"I'm glad you stopped by. Tell Robbie it's cool."

"Thanks for being so understanding." Brooke stood, leaving, but Colm didn't spare her a second glance.

Instead, he looked back at Kelli, who was obviously telling a heck of a story. Her hands were waving a mile a minute, and his two cousins were laughing so hard, they had tears in their eyes.

A light flashed on, and for a second, he swore he actually felt something inside go...click.

He glanced over to the bar. Rising, he walked across the room, stopping next to Pop Pop, right in front of Padraig.

"Where did you spend Halloween night?" Colm asked.

"What?" Padraig was clearly confused by the abrupt, odd question, but Colm needed to know.

"Halloween night. After the party. Where did you sleep?"

Padraig looked confused. "At my place. Emmy was my DD. She drove me home, got me into the apartment, poured me into bed, and then slept on the couch." He looked over at Emmy and smiled.

Emmy shrugged casually. "I was worried about him. So much bourbon."

"Lovely lass," Pop Pop said with a smile.

"Never again," Padraig promised her before looking back at Colm. "Why?"

"No reason."

All of Kelli's worrying, her guilt, had been for nothing. She hadn't been with Padraig.

She'd been with *him*.

All the pieces fell together, the puzzle complete.

Colm stood by the bar, trying to get himself together. He felt raw inside, ragged. Like he'd just gone twelve rounds with the heavyweight.

"Colm?" Pop Pop said.

At the same time, Padraig asked, "You okay, Bro?"

Colm considered the question...then felt a grin spread across his face. "Yeah. I'm good. I'm *really* fucking good."

"Language," Pop Pop murmured.

"Sorry, Pop Pop. I gotta go."

He walked away, leaving a confused twin and grandfather in his wake. He didn't stop until he was standing next to Kelli's table. "Hey, Kell. You got a second?"

"Sure." She rose quickly, no doubt curious about Brooke's reasons for stonewalling him the past week and a half.

He grasped her hand, leading her to the back of the pub.

"Where are we going?" she asked.

"Upstairs. Can't talk down here. Too loud."

"Okay. So what did Brooke say?" she asked as they climbed the stairs.

"Not yet," he said when they reached the top of the first flight.

Kelli started to walk toward the couch, but Colm pushed her toward the second set of stairs that would take her to his bedroom. "Keep going."

She paused for a moment, then shrugged nonchalantly,

climbing the stairs. "Not sure what's wrong with the living room. Everyone else is downstairs," she argued.

He didn't reply, just kept his hand on the small of her back, guiding her up the stairs, then turning her toward his room once they reached the top. And she didn't hesitate.

It spoke to their level of friendship, to the innate trust that existed between them, forged by thirty years of living within each other's space. He and Kelli had grown up together, seen each other through every single awkward phase of their lives. They'd eaten hundreds of school lunches at the same table, played a million different games, gone to concerts and football games, and too many bars to count. They'd laughed and fought like siblings and enemies—and friends.

"Colm?" she asked, as they entered his bedroom. "What the hell did she say? Why are you so worked up?"

He didn't answer. He couldn't.

It was Kelli.

It had been Kelli all along.

He shut the door and locked it.

She frowned. "What's wrong with you?"

He walked over to his dresser and picked up her panties, swinging them nonchalantly on his finger.

She realized what he had—and blushed. "Oh damn. Yeah. It occurs to me I probably should have told you something that...I forgot. Paddy and I were in *your* bed Halloween night. Did you just find those?" She was grinning now, clearly thinking he'd brought her up here to give her a hard time about sleeping with his brother in his bed.

She couldn't be more wrong.

She reached out, intent on taking them from him, but he closed his fist and held them away from her.

"Don't be a perv, Colm. That's my favorite pair of panties."

"They're mine now."

"Don't think they'll fit you," she joked.

"I took them off you Halloween night, Kell. Claimed them. They're mine."

"You...you didn't take them off me."

"Brooke wasn't in this room with me. She was next door. With *Robbie*."

"No. You were at Brooke's apartment. I saw you leave."

"We went downstairs to borrow a bottle of vodka from the pub because she was out. Told Brooke to meet me up here while I fixed the tap on the keg, but everyone was still playing that stupid game. Brooke didn't hear me whisper second door at the top of the stairs. She went to Finn's room."

"Your beard," she said, still fighting the truth. "It wasn't there."

"I shaved it off. It was the only way I could get the fake Hagrid one to stick to my face. You know me, in it to win it. I started growing it back the next day."

"I just thought you'd trimmed it too much." Colm watched her process what he was saying, and realized she was almost there when she said, "Paddy..."

"Spent the night happily passed out in his own bed. Think about it, Kell. He was way too wasted to do what *we* did that night."

Her shoulders drooped and for a second, she looked like a balloon someone had stuck a pin in, all the air seeping out of her. Then a huge smile filled her face. "Oh thank *God*.

This is amazing! I can't tell you how relieved I am. I mean... when I thought I'd...with Paddy. This has been *killing* me. It's like I can breathe for the first time in a week and a half!"

Colm leaned against his dresser and grinned, waiting for the other shoe to drop.

It didn't take too long.

"*Fuck*," she said, looking at him. "We had sex!"

"We had *good* sex."

"I don't want to talk about it."

Colm laughed. "Don't be shy, Kell. You can admit every single one of those orgasms were real, and then tell me I rocked your world. It won't be the first time I've heard it. I'm sure it won't be the last."

She gazed heavenward and closed her eyes. "Oh my God. Now I'm sorry I *didn't* sleep with Paddy." Then she started laughing. "And by the way, you owe me an apology. You said only I could manage to sleep with the wrong person."

Colm chuckled. "I stand corrected." Then, he couldn't resist poking a little fun. "You know, I'm really trying to remember your exact words last Friday." He tapped his lips as if thinking hard. "Think you called me a stud."

"I never said the word stud. Not once. Ever."

He shrugged. "It was definitely implied," he teased, enjoying the way she blushed.

Of course, it was Kelli, so he should have known it wouldn't take her too long to recover and manage to get in a dig of her own.

"Careful, hotshot. I was so good that night, you were ready to marry Brooke. Brooke, who never stops talking... about reality TV...and thinks throwing on a pink sweater and calling herself Regina George is a stellar Halloween costume. Think about that. Let it sink in. That's how hot *I* am in bed."

Colm didn't bother to admit that was all he'd been thinking about since Brooke dropped the bomb that it hadn't been her in his bed that night.

He walked over and sat on the edge of his bed, patting the mattress next to him. "Come here."

"Fuuuuuck no."

"I just want to talk to you."

"We can talk just like this."

"Chicken shit," he said, throwing her own taunt back at her.

It worked. Just like he'd known it would.

Kelli crossed over to him, sitting on the edge of his bed with one leg curled beneath her as she faced him. "What?" Her tone was hostile, but he knew it was a defensive move, so he didn't take offense.

He ran the back of his knuckles along her cheek, taking note of her soft intake of breath. "It's going to be okay, Kell. We're fine."

The storm clouds gathering in her expression as she prepared to go to battle lifted. "Yeah. Right. I mean...it's not like you and I are strangers to one-night stands. We'll just chalk it up to alcohol and bad decisions and move on."

He shook his head. "Nope. That's not happening."

"But you just said—"

"That we're fine. And we are."

Kelli was analyzing what had happened between them using historical data, taking everything she knew about him— his resistance to commitments, his sexual track record, his aversion to clingy women—and coming up with what she assumed would be a rock-solid conclusion.

That he wouldn't want more from her than just that one night.

That he wouldn't want to pursue anything serious.

She was wrong.

But Kelli wasn't a Collins. Which meant it was going to take her a little longer to catch up. To figure out what *he'd* just realized down in the pub.

The curse had struck.

And damn if it didn't have a sick sense of humor.

So he was going to give her time. But not much.

"I don't understand what you're saying."

"Why don't we take a few days?" he suggested. "Let the dust settle on this. You coming Sunday for football?"

She hesitated just long enough that he knew she was planning on avoiding him for a while. So he needed to put her on more solid ground, give her the Colm she was used to. It was a sneak attack on his part—but he played to win. Which was something Kelli knew very well but was probably going to forget in this instance.

He fought to school his features.

This was going to be fun.

"Let me rephrase that," he said. "You're coming for football on Sunday."

Kelli rolled her eyes. "You know that macho shit doesn't work with me."

"I don't know," he murmured. "I seem to recall something different on Halloween. You liked it when I spanked your ass. Oh...and I was right about the hair-pulling too."

She sighed. "You're going to be insufferable about this, aren't you?"

"Would you expect anything different?"

"How many years until I live this down?"

He chuckled. "All of them."

Indomitable soul that she was, she just grinned. "You're an asshole."

"And you're beautiful."

She froze, waiting for the punch line.

There wasn't one. He was overwhelmed by the desire to kiss her confusion away, to push her onto her back and show her exactly how things were going to play out from here...but Kelli wouldn't go down without a fight.

So he was going to take some time and figure out his game plan first.

When the silence stretched just a second too long, she glanced over his shoulder at the door. "I should...go."

He nodded, following suit as she stood up.

Kelli walked to the door and unlocked it, but he pushed it closed just as she started opening it.

"Turn around, Kelli."

She sighed, feigning annoyance, though he suspected what she really felt was nervousness. She twisted, her back pressed against the door, stealing every inch of distance she could manage from him.

"Aren't you forgetting something?" he asked.

"Thought you weren't giving me my panties back."

"My goodbye kiss."

Kelli rolled her eyes as he chuckled. He reached out and gave her a hug. She went stiff for just a moment, then her arms wrapped around his waist and she hugged him back, sighing.

"This should feel so weird," she whispered.

"But it doesn't." Colm gave her a platonic kiss on the top of the head. "We'll sort it all out. Don't worry."

It took everything he had to let her go and take a step back, but Kelli needed time to process. He knew she—like him—would relive Halloween night over countless times between now and Sunday, but in a different light. The things that hadn't made sense about that night *did* now. And they both needed time to put the memories together the right way, to let the emotions swirling around what they'd done emerge.

"See you Sunday," he said.

She nodded, turned, and left.

CHAPTER EIGHT

Kelli lay on her couch, staring at the ceiling. Her tiny Tortoiseshell cat, Mojo, was lying on her chest, purring peacefully. She'd been in this same position since dragging her ass out of bed this morning. It was Saturday, which was typically her get-shit-done day, but so far, the day had been a total bust.

She would pay for it next week when she ran out of clean socks and undies, but she couldn't make herself care too much about it right now.

Her mind was swimming in a sea of confused what-the-fuck-did-I-do and an ocean of I-want-more-Colm-sex.

The past two nights, she'd replayed Halloween night over and over in her mind until her body actually ached with physical need, and none of the vibrators in her extensive collection were doing a damn thing to help that situation.

Worst part was she couldn't figure out what *Colm* thought about any of it. He'd said they were fine, but then he'd said they weren't going to move on.

So...what did *that* mean?

Surely he didn't intend for them to have sex again?

Shit. She sort of hoped that was his intention. She wouldn't mind going in for another round or forty-seven, just to see if it was some sort of wine-induced fluke.

Of course, if they did sleep with each other, and it was amazing again, she'd still be fucked because it was Colm.

"I was a serial killer in a past life," she murmured. It was the only way she could explain how shit like this kept happening to her.

She'd meet a great guy she really liked, and inevitably there was always something wrong with him—he hated cats, he chain-smoked, he was lousy in bed.

And now, the one time she'd found a guy who seriously hit every freaking hot button in her body...it was Colm Collins.

Fuck. Me.

Her cell phone started ringing, and she considered letting it go to voicemail for a second.

"Sorry, Mojo," she said as she rolled toward the coffee table, forcing the cat to move. She picked up her cell, glancing at the caller ID. "Hey, Sunnie. What's up?"

"Just calling to make sure we're still on for dinner and party planning tonight."

Kelli jerked up off the couch and glanced at the clock. She hadn't even managed to shower or get dressed. It was nearly five o'clock, and she was still sporting bedhead and pajamas. "Shit. I forgot."

"Well, shake a leg, girlfriend. We've got work to do and margaritas to drink."

"I'm not drinking."

"We're going to a Mexican restaurant, Kell. Margaritas are nonnegotiable."

"You bet I'd fall off the wagon today in that pool of Colm's, didn't you?"

Sunnie laughed, not even bothering to feign innocence. "Day's not over yet, and he's got a pretty nice-size pot this year. Get a move on. Be there in an hour."

Sunnie didn't even bother to say goodbye or give Kelli a chance to make an excuse to get out of it. Not that she wanted to.

A girls' night out might just do the trick.

TWO HOURS LATER, Kelli was eyeballing the margaritas—the second round—in front of Darcy, Sunnie, and Yvonne, and regretting that she'd picked now to give up alcohol.

Because if she'd ever needed a drink...

Sunnie had her tablet open, going over everything one last time. "Okay, so Yvonne is making the cake, shaped like boobs, as well as the cake pops—don't forget the nipples on those. I love the idea of adding a bowlful of Mounds to the dessert table, Darc. Nicely played. And, Kelli, you sure you don't mind running to get the art supplies for the upcycling old bras contest."

Kelli nodded. "I'll make sure to have a good variety of crafty shit so people can really get creative."

They'd spent the last hour planning a Boob Voyage party for Darcy and Sunnie's godmother, Bubbles. Bubbles had been an "adopted" Collins since before any of them were born. According to Riley, she and Bubbles had been best friends since God was in diapers, the two of them meeting by chance in Vegas a million years ago.

Riley and Aaron had returned from Las Vegas the week after their elopement with Bubbles, a "former ho," as she liked to say, in tow. Since starting a new life in Baltimore, Bubbles had found work as an in-home caregiver for the elderly. She'd taken countless nursing classes over the years and currently lived in a detached apartment behind Riley and Aaron's house. She'd been a beloved member of the Collins family for years, and she was one of Kelli's favorite people on the planet.

The woman spoke her language. She never minced words and hadn't met a curse word she didn't love. It was Bubbles who had added the words cuntcake and twatwaffle to Kelli's vocabulary back when Kelli was in high school.

Bubbles was also extremely well-endowed. Like off-the-charts endowment. As such, she'd suffered with back pain for years, and a few months earlier, she'd decided it was time to reduce "the beasts," as she like to refer to them.

And, of course, the Collins clan considered that a reason to throw a party. Riley had put Kelli, Yvonne, Darcy, and Sunnie in charge of the food and games.

Kelli had to admit they'd come up with a pretty solid menu—including nippetizers like meatballs, chicken "breast" salad, and water*melon* salad. They planned to play "Pin the B-Cup on Bubbles," as well as award a prize for the most creative upcycle redesign using Bubbles' old bras. Sunnie also wanted to hold a contest to rename Bubbles, giving her a new, smaller-titty nickname.

The party was going to be a blast, but Kelli was struggling to work up any enthusiasm for it at the moment.

"So...now that *that's* all done," Sunnie said, turning off her tablet and twisting toward Kelli. "What the hell is wrong with you?"

Kelli reared back. "What do you mean?"

"You've been way too quiet tonight, and distracted, considering this is usually the type of thing you love."

She should have known Sunnie would pick up on her mood. Kelli considered the three women sitting with her some of her very best friends, the four of them spending countless happy hours and girls' nights out—like this one —together.

"There's a," Kelli waved her hand around, "thing going on right now and I need some advice. I kind of fucked up."

"Oh God. You finally broke down and told Princess Principal off, didn't you?" Yvonne said. "Are you fired?"

"No. I haven't snapped over that...yet. Though she tests me daily." Kelli's principal was a hypochondriac Prima Donna with a capital P *and* D, who flashed red hot or ice cold, depending on which of her many medications she did or did not take each morning.

"Well, if it's not work, than it's sex. Who did you fuck?" Sunnie asked.

Kelli shook her head and glanced heavenward. "Why does your mind always go straight to sex?"

Sunnie tilted her head in the ultimate know-it-all pose. "Am I wrong?"

"No."

"So I'll ask again. Who did you fuck?"

Kelli bit her lower lip and debated whether or not she should tell them—for about zero-point-four seconds—then she blurted it out because the truth was, she really did need their advice.

"Colm."

Kelli instantly regretted not having her phone out, videoing their responses. Because it wasn't often she was able to shock three Collins women into silence.

Sunnie, of course, recovered first. "Shut up. You did not!"

Kelli nodded slowly. "It was sort of an accident."

All three women burst into laughter as Darcy said, "Accident? So what happened? You slipped and fell on his dick?"

"I hate all of you," Kelli said even as she tried not to laugh. "I *really* need a drink."

Sunnie lit up and then raised her hand for the server. Kelli grabbed it and pulled it down.

"Forget it. I'm not caving just so you can win a bet. And it *was* an accident," she insisted to Darcy, "because I didn't know it was Colm."

"How can that even happen?"

Kelli crossed her arms. "There was a blackout."

"Halloween? The two of you had sex on *Halloween*, and we're just now hearing about it?" Yvonne picked up her drink and took a big sip. "I can't believe you held out on us that long."

"I only just found out I was with Colm Thursday night, at karaoke. I thought I'd slept with Robbie...and then..." She stopped right there, deciding to omit the Padraig part of the story.

"But Colm must have known," Darcy said.

Kelli shook her head. "He thought he was with Brooke."

Yvonne frowned, clearly struggling to make sense of it all. "I know it was super dark, but surely you recognized each other's voices."

Kelli shot Sunnie a dirty look. "We were still playing your stupid *Quiet Place* game."

Sunnie laughed, completely unrepentant. "Oh my God! Do I know how to throw a party or what? Just when I think I can't top myself—boom, Kelli and Colm hook up and don't even realize it. I might just hang it all up now and rest on my laurels because there's no beating *that*."

"What about the Boob Voyage?" Yvonne reminded her cousin.

"And Friendsgiving?" Darcy added.

"Damn. Yeah. Okay. I'll hang up my hat after the holiday season." Sunnie lifted her margarita glass, but put it down again, leaning closer to Kelli. "So, how was it?"

"Seriously, Sun? He's your cousin."

Sunnie shrugged, and Kelli knew the other woman wasn't going to give up. She was as nosy as the rest of her family, and she loved a good sex story. "So what? Details or it never happened."

"I'm not giving you details."

"You said you needed advice," Yvonne—God bless her— said, changing the subject. "What's going on?"

"Please tell me my cousin isn't acting like a total douchebag about it." From her tone, it was clear Sunnie would give Colm shit if he was.

Kelli shook her head. "No. He's cool. I mean, we talked about it and we're okay."

Darcy studied her face. "So if you're both cool with it, and you still need advice..."

Sunnie's eyes widened. "You want to sleep with him again, don't you?"

Kelli's knee-jerk reaction was to deny that assertion immediately—but she couldn't.

"Holy shit, Kell," Sunnie said, letting Kelli's silence provide the answer. "He was *that* good?"

Kelli rolled her eyes. "If I said yes—and mind you, I'm not saying that, I'm only asking out of curiosity—how much shit would you guys give me and for how long?"

Sunnie leaned back and pretended to consider the question. "That's a tough one. Because, damn, there's just so much material to use."

Kelli sighed heavily, but Sunnie was only just getting going.

"I mean, a picture is starting to form of you and Colm in bed together. I can almost see him playing the cocky macho card the entire time, pissing you off, while he loses his shit every time you tell him what he's doing wrong and how to correct it."

Darcy and Yvonne both tried to hide their giggles behind their hands.

Kelli would love to be annoyed by this whole conversation, but the truth was...it was exactly what she needed. She'd been too in her head the past couple of days, worrying about something that really, actually, was pretty funny.

At least on the surface.

If she could just focus on the humor of the situation, she'd have already forgotten and moved on. But...she couldn't let go of the way it felt to be held by him, the way he kissed her as if he couldn't get enough, the way he slid deep inside, filling her, touching places she hadn't even known existed.

Everything Sunnie had said about their personalities and the way she and Colm had always communicated in the past was true, so she wasn't wrong to think that would carry over to the bedroom.

Except it hadn't.

Of course, he'd thought she was Brooke. What if that was why it had been so great? And who was to say that if they decided to have sex again, it wouldn't turn out exactly as Sunnie described? They'd taken talking...and vision...off the table the other night. That wouldn't be the case if they went back for seconds. "So what you're saying is, forget it. It'll never work."

Sunnie sobered up, and for the first time, Kelli could see her friend was suddenly taking her seriously. "No," she said after a moment of reflection. "I'm not. It's obvious something happened between you two that night. Something that's shaken you up a little. And I'm glad."

"You're glad I'm shaken up?"

Sunnie nodded. "Yeah. You needed to have your foundation rocked. I don't think that's happened to you in a very long time. If ever. And the thing is...that's what makes life worth living."

Kelli hadn't considered that, but she could see now that Sunnie was right. She'd merely been existing the past year or...maybe decade. Stuck in a rut, miserable, lonely.

Sunnie ran her finger around the rim of her margarita glass, sucking the sugar off the tip as she thought. "If you'd had amazing sex with any other guy in the world, you'd be going back for seconds, right?"

Kelli nodded. "And thirds. And fourths. And—"

"Wow. Go Colm," Darcy murmured.

"So why aren't you going for that now?" Yvonne asked.

"You all think I should just go with the flow? With *Colm?*" she stressed.

Yvonne nodded and smiled. "Yes. That's exactly what you should do."

"And when it blows up in my face?"

Yvonne rolled her eyes. "Always so negative, Eeyore. Always waiting for things to fall apart."

"Because they always do!"

"Until they don't," Yvonne added. "And then...it's perfect, and completely worth the risk."

"Spoken like a true Collins." Kelli smiled as she said it, then considered their advice, realizing she hadn't given them all the facts.

Kelli hadn't told her girlfriends about wanting a baby. She wasn't sure why she was holding that part back.

This whole conversation was probably moot because the fact still remained that she still wanted to move forward with the baby plan.

Though she didn't have a clue exactly how that was going to happen at the moment. Colm hadn't been on her original list and he still wasn't because she knew he and Padraig had more in common than just looks. Colm wouldn't "gift" her sperm and walk away, and things between them were complicated enough without adding a baby wrinkle to things.

And now she was worried about Robbie's participation because she didn't have a clue what was going on between him and Brooke.

Regardless of all of that, her decision to have a baby had been made months ago, and it was rock solid. Her wild night with Colm hadn't changed that at all.

Which should have made walking away from Colm very, *very* simple.

She'd sworn off men, determined to focus on getting pregnant, on motherhood, on setting her feet on a path she knew—beyond a shadow of a doubt—would bring her happiness.

The same couldn't be said of Colm. She was a relationship disaster. He was a commitment-phobe, determined to fuck his way freely all the way to forty.

And that was just separately. Together, they were oil and water, Harry and Voldemort, Hamilton and Burr.

In truth, the whole thing was a no-brainer. Shake off the one-night stand with Colm and move on, move forward.

So why *wasn't* it simple?

CHAPTER NINE

"Alright! They did it!" Kelli high-fived Colm, both of them grinning widely over the Ravens' big win.

"They're going all the way to the Super Bowl this year," Colm said. "I can feel it in my bones."

The two of them stood up, stretching after sitting through the game and overtime. Kelli did a little victory dance, bumping her hip against Colm's as she laughed. She looked adorable in the Ravens jersey he and Paddy had bought her for Christmas a couple of years ago. She was as big a die-hard fan as anyone in his family...and that was saying something.

Of course, when he considered it, it made sense. She'd been watching Sunday football with his family for close to two decades.

He'd been way too happy when she'd arrived a few hours earlier, chips and dip in hand, just like always, grabbing a seat with him and his cousins, ready to watch the game.

Colm considered it a victory that she'd shown up

without him having to go get her. Now it was time to scale the second wall because, while she was here, she was working overtime to resume their previous trash-talking frenemies relationship.

Kelli was about to figure out there was a new norm.

He watched as she started gathering up the dirty paper plates and empty beer cans. Knowing her, she was a few minutes away from saying goodbye and trying to escape, but her good manners wouldn't let her leave without offering to tidy up.

"What do you say we go down to the pub and celebrate with Pop Pop and Guinness?" Oliver suggested. The youngest of Colm's cousins, the poor boy had spent too many years longing to be a part of the older cousins' group, bemoaning the fact it had taken him forever to turn twenty-one so he could start hanging out at the pub with them. Unfortunately, now that he'd finally arrived at legal age, the cousins he'd wanted to go club-hopping with were now married and starting families.

Colm felt sorry for the kid—as the family called him, much to Oliver's annoyance—and tried to pick up the slack as much as he could. Not that it was a hardship. Oliver was exactly like his father, Sean. Laid-back, up for anything, live and let live. He was quick to laugh, told great stories, and had never met a stranger.

Of course, Colm figured that probably described at least half the members of the Collins clan.

Gavin, Oliver's best friend and foster brother, stood up immediately, all in. He grabbed the empty wings platter, nothing left but a pile of bones and globs of barbeque sauce, and carried it to the kitchen.

"Sounds like a great idea," Kelli said, as she continued to clean up.

Colm grinned. She was taking great care, making sure they didn't end up alone together.

She was going to lose that battle.

She'd been sitting next to Colm on the couch all afternoon, their legs pressed against each other's as they shared the space with Oliver, Gavin in one recliner, Darcy—who'd left at halftime for some reason she didn't seem willing to share—in the other chair.

Once Darcy left, Oliver claimed her spot, but he and Kelli hadn't separated, hadn't put so much as an inch between themselves.

He wondered if she was feeling the pull. Now that the truth about Halloween was out, Colm was hard-pressed to resist the need to—God—have her near him, to touch her.

"Kelli and I will clean up and meet you guys down there in a little while," Colm said, spying a way to steal a few minutes alone with her.

Kelli flashed him a suspicious look but didn't reject the idea.

Oliver and Gavin—no fans of housework—took them up on the deal.

"See you in a few," Oliver said over his shoulder as they walked downstairs to the pub.

Kelli grabbed some more trash and carried it to the kitchen. He followed her with the roll of paper towels and half-eaten bag of chips.

They tidied up a few things in the kitchen, then Kelli grabbed a wet dishcloth and headed back to the living room to wipe up the coffee table.

Colm grabbed the dishcloth away from her just as she exited the kitchen and pitched it back toward the sink.

"Hey," she started, but she stopped when he took her hand and dragged her into the bathroom.

"What..." That was all Kelli bothered to say when Colm shut the door and locked it.

And that was the end of her resistance.

She met him halfway, the two of them kissing like their lives depended on it.

Colm grasped her waist, pushing her back toward the sink as Kelli wrapped her arms around his shoulders, her hands in his hair.

He hadn't kissed her since Halloween, but damn if he hadn't spent every single fucking night since Thursday dreaming about doing this again. He pressed her lips open, dipping his tongue inside her mouth for a taste.

Barbeque sauce and ranch dip.

Spicy, the perfect combination. She was delicious, and her lips soft despite the definite urgency of the kiss. She wanted this as much as he did.

Colm reached for the bottom of her jersey, only breaking the kiss for the three seconds it took to pull the thing over her head. He tossed it to the floor.

Kelli fisted his T-shirt in her hands, pulling him back to her, kissing him again.

Colm slipped his hands behind her back and, with practiced fingers, unfastened her bra with one quick flip.

"I'm going to ignore how fucking good you are at that," she murmured, her lips still on his.

Colm chuckled, even as they continued to kiss. He drew

the bra straps over her shoulders, tugging the lacy material away and dropping it to the floor with her jersey.

He lifted her so that she was sitting on the sink, her thighs outstretched. He stepped between them, certain she could feel his erection pressing against her, even through the denim of both their jeans.

Part of him kept waiting for her to come to her senses, to stop him.

When Kelli wrapped her legs around his hips and pressed her crotch more firmly against his, it occurred to Colm she had the same fear.

Afraid he'd call a halt.

No. Fucking. Way.

They kissed for several more minutes, their hands exploring, stroking, caressing. He'd thought Halloween night was hot, the way he'd had to rely on only his sense of touch, blinded by the darkness.

Seeing her was a million times better. She was sexy, curvy. Her skin was flushed a beautiful rosy red that covered her cheeks and crept along her neck and chest. He wouldn't have expected that almost innocent reaction from her.

He played with her breasts, squeezing them, pinching her nipples, loving the way she gasped and moaned and arched her back, inviting him to take more.

"I love your tits, Kell. God. They're perfect."

He felt her smile, rather than saw it, when he immediately resumed the kiss.

Kelli's hands had drifted beneath his T-shirt, her thumbs toying with his nipples, her nails lightly scratching his chest, playing with the smattering of hair there.

He released one of her breasts, reaching up to take a handful of her hair in his hand. He closed his fist around the long auburn strands, tugging until she groaned with pleasure.

He'd heard those same sounds from her on Halloween, and now he wondered how he hadn't realized it was her. Her groans, her sighs, her hisses when...

He grinned when she gave him one of those sharp sounds as he pulled her hair harder, drawing her head back so he could deepen the kiss.

Kelli, the gorgeous, impatient woman, took them to the next level, her fingers flipping open the button on his jeans with ease.

"I'm going to ignore how good you are at that," he murmured, repeating her words.

She pulled away from him, laughing softly as she tugged his zipper down. Reaching into his open jeans, she wrapped her hand around his cock.

"Going commando, I see."

He winked, loving her easy smile and the way she rolled her eyes at him.

Kelli had probably rolled her eyes a million times in his presence, typically in annoyance over something he said that she found offensive or arrogant. The devil in him had always enjoyed provoking that response from her, loved tweaking her, teasing her, giving her shit.

Never, not once, had it made him this hard, made him lose his mind with desire, with need.

This time...

"God, Kelli." Her impatience rubbed off on him as he took one small step back, drawing her off the sink so he could divest her of her jeans. She helped him, shimmying them and her panties down her hips, before she kicked them off with her shoes.

He opened the drawer next to her, rummaging to the back, finding the stash of condoms he and Oliver kept there "for emergencies."

Kelli had shoved his jeans to his knees and resumed her place on the sink, using her legs to draw him back to her.

Halloween had been hours of foreplay and fondling, but it was clear neither of them was interested in a repeat performance of that. At least not this time.

Colm had spent too many nights alone with just his hand since then.

He opened the condom wrapper and started to pull it on. He'd just covered the tip when Kelli stopped him.

He looked up, catching her tentative—confused?—gaze.

He shook his head. "That's a lot longer conversation, Kell."

Her hand dropped away as she nodded hastily. "You're right. It is."

"And we're going to have it." Colm finished rolling on the condom, wondering if she'd stop him now. If the magic had somehow been broken.

He should have known better.

Kelli was indomitable, unshakable. Amazing.

She guided his cock to the opening of her body.

He wiggled his thumb over her clit. She was wet. So damn wet.

Her eyes drifted closed when he pressed the head inside.

"No," he said, more loudly than he'd intended.

Her eyes flew open, met his.

"Don't close your eyes. I want to make *damn* sure you know exactly who you're with this time."

She laughed, just one brief huff of amusement, before he thrust in. Straight to the hilt.

Kelli threw her head back as they found their rhythm in seconds. She added her own strength to his, using her legs to pull him back inside her every time he retreated.

They came together in a rush as he moved in and out in an almost brutal fashion.

Kelli drove him on, demanding more. Always more.

"Wait!" she cried out when he completely withdrew.

"No. Turn around." He already had her halfway to the position he wanted before he finished speaking, bending her over the sink, pulling her ass toward him.

He shoved back in roughly, loving the way she cried out, "Yes. God! *Yes!*"

Colm watched her face in the reflection of the mirror, her gaze locked on his as well.

Over and over, he took her. It was hard and fast and practically primal. When her cheeks flushed a deeper red and her breathing grew erratic, he knew she was close.

Colm slowed his thrusts as he bent over her back, his lips by her ear. "Don't hold back, Kelli. I want to watch you come."

She started to nod, but he wasn't finished.

"But just know I'm not stopping. I'm gonna keep fucking you all the way through your orgasm. I'm going to make sure it lasts, going to draw it out until it hurts, until you're *begging* me to stop."

Kelli shuddered, though the response couldn't be

mistaken as anything other than pure hunger. "Please," she whispered.

"Then I'm going to make you do it all over again when *I* come."

She was gasping for air, and Colm could swear he almost saw her trying to prepare herself, trying to get ready for exactly what he promised.

He couldn't hold back his grin, couldn't keep it from growing when she narrowed her eyes. He was still moving inside her, but it was too slow to push her over.

Teasing her was second nature to him, something he'd always loved, but now, bringing it here, to this...

His eyes had been opened. And he'd never seen anything more perfect.

"All talk, Colm?" she asked breathlessly. "No action?"

He chuckled, making sure to infuse a warning in the sound. "Always poking the bear."

"At least someone in this room is pok—"

That was as much of the joke as she managed. Colm slammed into her roughly, his fingers gripping her hips so tight, he knew she was going to bruise. He liked the idea of that, wanted her wearing his marks, wearing a reminder of exactly how he'd taken her.

Maybe it would even help her realize who he was going to be to her.

She didn't yet.

But she would soon.

Kelli's cries grew louder, and he hoped Oliver and Gavin stayed down in the pub, ordered a second round—maybe even a third.

Her orgasm struck hard, and Colm clenched his teeth so tightly, he worried about breaking his own jaw.

"*Jesus.*" He'd told her what he was going to do, but there was nothing like the feeling of Kelli coming on his dick, her orgasm squeezing him so tight, it wasn't just *her* who was feeling the pain.

Kelli trembled as her orgasm started to wane, her head falling forward, hiding her face.

He reached up and grasped her hair, drawing her head back up so he could see her eyes reflected in the mirror once more.

Colm wasn't gentle about it. Not that he needed to worry. Kelli's back arched into the strong grip and—fuck him —she came again. This one even harder than the first.

She called out his name, the single syllable broken, beautiful. "Colm!"

This time, he slowed his pace. It was the only way he could regain control, could hold off his own imminent climax.

Kelli shuddered and shook as the last vestiges of her orgasm faded. He watched her face through it all and knew he'd *never* see anything more beautiful.

Releasing her hair, he gently rubbed her scalp. Then he pulled out.

Kelli lifted her head, her gaze connecting with his in the mirror.

He wrapped his hand around her elbow, drawing her up and turning her to face him again. Lifting her to her original position, he guided his cock back to her pussy.

Colm kissed her as he slowly pressed back inside.

Kelli broke the kiss, seeking air. "I just..." She shivered. "I don't think I can do that—"

"Shhh. Just one more, Kell. One more with me."

This time, he built his pace slowly, giving her time to recover, to let the sensations spark again. When he felt her hips lift to meet him, he knew she was back. She was ready.

He cupped her ass, pulling her closer to the edge of the sink. Then he gave in to his baser desires once more—fucking her, claiming her, possessing her. Making love to her.

Kelli's hands gripped his hips, his incredible, demanding woman, jerking him to her as if she simply couldn't get enough. Never enough.

She flew over the edge, and he followed her, locking his knees, fighting to remain upright as lightning struck.

He came harder than he thought possible, her body milking every single drop of come from him.

For several minutes—or maybe hours—they remained there, connected, struggling to breathe, fighting to still their racing hearts.

Finally, he found the strength to push away, to pull out of her. He threw the condom away, then reached for a washcloth as Kelli sat, motionless, watching him.

He wet the cloth with warm water and ran it along her slit gently before cleaning himself as well.

Colm watched as the fog of lust lifted and the awareness he'd been waiting for arrived.

"That was," she paused, then forged on, "a mistake."

It wasn't. But Colm knew she wouldn't accept that from him. Not yet. So he kept quiet.

She didn't seem to notice his silence as she continued, "We can't do that again."

He let his cocky grin tell her exactly what he thought of that assertion, and she rolled her eyes.

"I'm being serious, Colm."

"I know you are."

"I'm sorry I tried to...stop you from...putting on the condom."

He wasn't used to seeing Kelli as anything other than one hundred percent confident, so it was obvious he'd drawn her way beyond her comfort zone. "It's okay. I think we should talk about it."

She considered that, then shook her head. "No. There are mistakes, and then there are *mistakes*."

Colm was going to love every second of that particular mistake, but unlike him, his girl hadn't opened her eyes, hadn't let herself see what was happening here.

"That was..." She blew out a long breath, and he knew she didn't want to admit what she was about to say. However, Kelli never shied away from the truth. Even if it meant being nice to him. "Fucking incredible."

He laughed. "How much did that hurt to say?"

"A lot, so don't expect me to repeat it."

He gave her a soft kiss on the cheek and then, because he couldn't resist, he enveloped her in a big hug. One she sank into without reservation.

Progress.

CHAPTER TEN

K elli glanced down at her hand linked with Colm's as they walked along the quiet city streets. It wasn't too late, only a little past nine, but the Collins Friendsgiving had ended earlier than usual.

She could only assume everyone was still recovering from Halloween two weeks earlier.

"I was surprised to see Ryder there," Colm observed.

"Yeah. Me too. I know Darcy and Yvonne invite him to pretty much everything, but the guy is a serious workaholic, so..."

"Guess that made Darcy happy. She's got a hell of a crush on the man."

Kelli grinned. "She wouldn't be happy to hear you refer to it as a crush."

"The guy is ten years older than her, *and* her boss. She's his babysitter, for God's sake. That makes it a crush."

Kelli shook her head. "Don't think any of that matters to Darc. She's got it for him bad."

"Which is a shame, because I don't think Ryder can see beyond the end of the cell phone that's constantly in his hand long enough to realize."

She stopped walking. "You're joking, right? Were you not paying attention tonight?"

Colm gave her a confused look. "Paying attention to what?"

"Ryder was looking at Darcy like she was a chocolate cake. And he wasn't sharing it with *anybody*."

She instantly regretted her comment when Colm scowled. She dropped his hand and raised her own quickly. "Oh no you don't."

"Don't what?" he asked, his tone a bit darker than it had been before.

"You and Paddy and those Neanderthal cousins of yours don't need to start circling the wagons around sweet, innocent Darcy. She's fine."

And with that statement, she'd gone from sticking her foot in her mouth to swallowing all the way up to her knee.

"Innocent?" Colm sounded more curious.

She waved him off and started walking again. "Forget it."

"She's still a virgin, isn't she? I have to admit, I always wondered. She's never had a sleepover with a guy at the apartment, and she's lived there nearly three years."

"We're not talking about that. I'm sure there's a girlfriend code, and I'd rattle off the legal number to you if I knew it."

Colm chuckled, then mercifully let the subject drop.

"Ollie and Gavin weren't their usual loud, boisterous, frat-boy selves," she observed, determined to make sure Colm dropped the Darcy conversation for good.

"Yeah. I noticed. They've been quiet the last couple of

days. Ollie met a girl, and I think he really likes her. I get the impression Gavin is jealous."

"He likes her too?"

Colm had reclaimed her hand, but this time, it was he who pulled them to a stop. "I think Gavin is jealous of the *girl*."

Kelli let that sink in. "Ollie and Gavin? No. They're just friends, brothers even."

"You don't live in the Collins Dorm full-time like I do. I've seen some things that make me think the 'just friends' line has been crossed a few times. I mean, it's not like they're a couple, but...I don't know. There's something there."

"Wow. I had no idea. They both go out on dates with girls all the time."

"Yeah, but look at how they were raised. Three parents. Sean and Chad are bi, and as much with each other as they are Aunt Lauren. If Ollie's said it once, he's said it a million times. He wants a marriage just like his parents have."

"And he's picked Gavin as part of that threesome?"

"Gavin's been a part of that family since he was eleven years old. Maybe he wants the same thing."

"Maybe, but..." Kelli wasn't as convinced.

"But what?" Colm prompted.

"I've had a few conversations with just Gavin, and I don't get the impression he wants that at all."

She and Colm started walking again, both of them quiet. She suspected Colm was digesting that information, weighing it against his own opinions. He'd always been an introspective guy, even back in school. While she and Padraig were more verbal, typically expressing every thought the second they had it, Colm was quieter, and when he spoke, his thoughts were fully formed and measured.

The second she thought his name, she said it aloud—proving she hadn't changed much from when she was younger.

"Paddy."

Colm sighed. "Yeah."

Those two words proved just how in synch Colm and Kelli were when it came to Padraig.

"We knew this was coming, Kell."

She nodded. She had. Padraig had been very quiet at Friendsgiving, withdrawn. Too many times, she'd caught sight of that vacant, faraway look in his eyes. The one he always managed to shutter away and hide when he realized she was looking at him. Then he'd paste on a fake smile that didn't fool her one bit and give her a wink she was certain he thought set her mind at ease.

It didn't.

"I miss Mia," she whispered, her voice breaking slightly. She hadn't said those words—hadn't even allowed herself to think them—in a long time, because the second she did, a heavy weight settled on her chest and she usually wound up crying herself to sleep.

"So do I. I miss my brother too," Colm confessed.

Kelli turned her face away, trying to wipe away a tear without him seeing. He didn't let her get away with it. Using the grip on her hand, he tugged her toward him, wrapping her up in a big, strong hug, giving her a second to get herself under control.

They didn't say anything more. The past two years, they'd said it all...a thousand times. Talked until they were hoarse, trying to figure out how to heal Padraig's shattered heart. It was the only time the two of them waved the white flag and called a truce, speaking about something that genuinely worried them both, though Kelli hadn't realized that was what they were doing until just now. The moments when they talked about Padraig were the only times she'd felt some level of solidarity with Colm prior to Halloween.

And this was the first time Colm had ever hugged her after one of these talks, ever offered comfort through touch rather than words.

His silent strength soaked in deeper than anything he could ever say. She sucked in several deep breaths, squeezing him tighter for a second before releasing him. She looked up, giving him a weak attempt at a smile. "Thanks. I needed that."

He cupped her cheek affectionately, giving her the same sad smile. "So did I."

Then he bent lower and kissed her. It was a soft, sweet, gentle touch of his lips against hers, but it packed a punch. It didn't last more than a few seconds, then he pressed his forehead to hers and gave her his signature cocky-ass grin. "We're here."

Kelli straightened and looked over her shoulder at her apartment building. "You know, you didn't have to walk me home. I could have grabbed an Uber."

"I needed to walk off that dinner. We haven't even hit Thanksgiving and I've already packed on a couple extra pounds."

Colm was built like most of the men in his family, tall with broad shoulders. Colm's mom, Lane, referred to their dad, Tris, as Everest, and his sons had definitely acquired that same mountainous physique. Not that any of it was fat. Colm and Padraig both belonged to a boxing club and it ensured they were made of pure muscle.

Kelli released his hand. "Well, I guess I should—"

"Invite me up." There wasn't a hint of request in his words, so of course, it tweaked Kelli just enough that she'd deny herself what she wanted—him in her bed tonight—just to put the man in his place.

"I don't think that's a good idea."

Though the two of them had gone out for dinner a couple of nights this week, they'd met at the restaurants and managed to not talk about Halloween...or that fucking hot-as-shit interlude in the bathroom last Sunday.

"Kell," he said, his gaze heated...hungry. "Invite me up. *Now.*"

"You know," she said, turning away from him, not surprised when he followed, "it would serve you right if I sent you packing, you cocky bastard."

"But then you'd suffer too."

She glanced over her shoulder to make sure he could see her rolling her eyes. "I'd hardly suffer. You're not that—"

Colm cut her words off with a firm smack on the ass. "You go to hell for lying, Kell." And then, to punctuate that, he smacked her again.

"Ouch," she said through clenched teeth, trying not to recall how he'd done the same thing the night of Halloween —and how much she'd fucking loved it. She punched in the code to her apartment building and led him inside.

"That was just a warm-up," he warned.

He'd certainly warmed up her ass, but she wasn't about to admit that. Or how much she wanted him to make it burn.

Somehow the asshole knew because he gave her an amused chuckled, wrapping his arm around her waist to tug her closer as they walked up the first flight of stairs. She lived on the third floor of the apartment building, and the elevator only worked about a quarter of the time. As such, Kelli never used it, calling the two flights of stairs her workout routine. Well, that and seven daily hours of chasing a bunch of five-year-olds.

Yeah. Her exercise regime was solid, she thought sarcastically. Unlike Colm, who was rock-hard all over, she was a bit more plush...or as one of her students, Nykeya, liked to say, fluffy.

Unlocking her door, they hadn't made it more than two steps over the threshold before Colm was kicking it shut with his foot. He quickly threw the dead bolt, then reached for her.

She met him halfway, the two of them kissing like he'd been off to war for years. All freaking day, she'd felt this damn pull, fighting like the devil not to push him into some empty bedroom and rip off his clothes.

His brother and cousins would have loved that. Though Sunnie, Yvonne, and Darcy wouldn't have been too surprised.

Sunnie had pulled her aside at one point and threatened to turn the hose on her and Colm if they gave off any more sparks.

Kelli had brushed it off, but there was no denying the truth of her words. Kelli had been on a slow simmer all day, and now...

Now it was a full-blown boil.

A meow caught her attention, and she looked down to

find Mojo rubbing against Colm's legs.

"Hey, Mojo," he said, acknowledging her cat in a way that was pretty adorable, before he pulled off his jacket, leaving it on the floor. Then did the same with hers.

Colm slowly started pushing her backwards, down the hallway to her bedroom, all the time kissing her like his life depended on it. She worked the buttons of his shirt free, moving so fast that at one point, she heard the slight tearing of fabric.

Colm's hands had pulled her top from her jeans and slipped beneath, using his large grip to stroke the sensitive skin of her midsection, even as he steadied her on her backwards trek toward the bedroom.

Once his shirt hung open, she ran her fingers down his chest, stealing a quick touch before she started tackling his belt. She unthreaded it from the loops with a sharp swish, just as they reached her bedroom door.

Colm's hands had found their way to her bra, beneath her shirt, and he was cupping her breasts firmly, squeezing them, pinching her nipples through the lace. Through it all, he'd never once broken the kiss.

"God," she breathed when the back of her knees hit the edge of her mattress. Colm pulled her shirt over her head in one quick motion, drawing her bra straps over her shoulders to place kisses there. He was just about to push her down when Kelli caught sight of her messy bed, and she remembered...

"Shit," she whispered, pushing against Colm, trying to back him up. She'd have been more successful shoving a skyscraper.

"What's wrong?" he murmured, his lips traveling over

her cheek and down the side of her neck. Her eyes drifted closed for just a second before they flew open again.

"I need to make the bed," she blurted out.

Colm lifted his head away from the shoulder he'd started to lick and gave her a funny look. "That is the definition of pointless."

"Yeah, but...um...I'd still like to straighten up in here a little. I wasn't expecting you to come back with me."

He glanced around her far-too-tidy room. God, why was she such a neat freak?

Then his gaze drifted to her bed—and he grinned.

The sheets were twisted to hell. She'd spent every single night this week trying to work off some arousal.

"What's in the bed?" he asked.

She scowled, hoping to wipe the know-it-all look off his face. Of course the son of a bitch would know exactly why she was suddenly panicking. "Nothing," she lied, though her denial was the *true* definition of pointless.

"Tell me," he urged her.

Kelli sighed...trying to guess herself. Typically, she washed and packed her toys away afterwards, but she'd been so hot and bothered last night, knowing she was going to see Colm today, that she'd really expanded her usual workout routine, then passed out in exhaustion afterwards. Sadly, none of it had held a candle to what she knew he could do to her.

She turned toward the bed.

"Come on, Kell. What's hiding in those sheets?"

Oh, fuck it. He wasn't going anywhere until she told him. "An oral sex simulator, one—possibly two—vibrators, and a dildo."

Colm burst out laughing. "Jesus. I'm really getting to you, aren't I?"

"Hate to burst your bubble, but Chris Hemsworth is my go-to."

Colm wrapped his arms around her from behind, placing one of those right-on-the-erogenous-zone kisses to the nape of her neck, and she melted. "You can call me Thor later."

"Go home." There was no heat behind her words, and God help her if he called her bluff.

"Nope. You and I are going on a treasure hunt."

She considered repeating her request that he leave with a little more gusto, then mentally kicked her own ass.

Was she seriously going to turn down a night with Colm, a bed, and an array of sex toys?

Fuck no.

Colm stepped around her and threw back the duvet, laughing. "Wow. You might be the woman of my dreams."

"Might be?" she asked, pretending to be offended. She pointed to the bed. "That's hot and you know it."

He reached for her G-spot vibrator, waving it in front of her. "This looks like it has potential. And what is an oral sex stimulator?"

"The name doesn't say it all? Meet Ora." She reached for her Ora, handing it to him. Then she crossed her fingers to form a hashtag. "Hashtag who needs men?" she joked.

He studied it, then turned it on. His eyes widening. "Nice. But I'm going to make you eat those words. Grab the other vibrator and the dildo and follow me."

Colm led her to the bathroom, shaking his head as he washed off her vibrators. "You should take better care of your toys."

Kelli watched him, struggling not to laugh at the outright absurdity of the situation. Was she seriously standing in her bathroom in her bra as Colm washed her vibrators and...

He held up the dildo he'd taken from her and blew out a long breath. "Couldn't find a bigger one?" The question was pure sarcasm.

"Sunnie gave it to me as a gag gift for my birthday a couple years ago. I whip it out every now and then because I like a challenge."

He studied it for a second longer, then pitched it to the corner. "Yeah well, tonight the only big hammer coming to bed with us is the one in my pants."

"Intimidated?"

He ignored her as he scooped up the vibrators and her Ora and they returned to her room.

"Take off your clothes."

"So demanding," she murmured, even as she unhooked her bra and slid it off. She stripped off her jeans and panties. Once she was naked, she gestured toward him. "Your turn."

He dropped the toys on the bed, then tugged off the shirt she'd already unbuttoned, his jeans going next.

"Still going commando, huh?"

"Worked late a few days this week. Missed laundry day. Lay down on the bed. You're going to give me a toy demonstration."

Kelli climbed onto her bed, shaking her head. "If I wanted to play with my toys, you wouldn't be here."

He picked up the oral sex simulator, then crawled onto the bed, pressing her to her back and caging her beneath him.

Kelli wrapped her arms around his neck and pulled him

toward her for a kiss. She was becoming somewhat addicted to Colm's kisses. He held his weight on his elbows as he kissed her senseless. The man really took his time with her lips, stroking them with his tongue, giving her playful nips. He didn't rush them along to the next part, like most of the men in her past.

She'd never met a guy who considered kissing serious foreplay. Not like Colm did. She ran her hands through his hair, then stroked his beard. She hadn't dated many men with facial hair, either, and she liked the extra sensation it provided.

She giggled softly when he slowly broke the kiss, his lips trailing over her cheek.

"Something funny?" he murmured, drifting to her ear, sucking on the lobe for a second before moving down to her neck.

"Your beard tickles," she whispered.

"I'd shave it off, but I've been told I can't pull off the beardless look as well as Paddy. Something to do with my mouth."

She laughed breathlessly for a second before the sound turned to a gasp. Colm was currently putting that mouth to very good use, licking her nipple.

"God. So good." She tried to hold his face to her breast, but Colm clearly had a different plan. He kept moving south, until he knelt between her outstretched thighs.

Her eyes had drifted closed, but they flew open when she heard a buzzing sound just a second before Colm held the Ora against her clit.

"Oh my God!" Her hips lifted of their own accord, trying to seek out more stimulation. Colm had quickly bypassed the slower speeds, going straight for the kill. She'd treated herself to the expensive toy last Christmas, deciding she wanted higher-tech, better orgasms. The cheap toys just weren't cutting it anymore.

Colm was wielding the thing like a professional, driving her to the edge of a climax in less than a minute.

Just before she could catch it, though, he turned the toy off.

"No. Wait!" She tried to pull it back to herself, but Colm tossed it to the foot of the bed, out of her reach. "Dammit, Colm."

He lowered his head, his breath hot on her sensitive, very wet pussy. He didn't say a word as he ran his tongue along her slit.

"Fuck," she breathed, her body trembling as he sucked her clit in his mouth roughly. Mercifully, Colm was smart enough to grip her hips before his attack, otherwise she might have hurt him with her wild gyrations.

He sucked harder, then wiggled his tongue against her clit.

"Who taught you that?" she cried.

Colm chuckled, the response only adding more vibration to her already overstimulated clit.

"Shit!" She came hard, her bones rattling with the impact. A meteor striking the planet wouldn't have shaken her with this much intensity.

Colm was a fucking clit master.

She struggled to catch her breath, as Colm rose up until he was kneeling once again. As her wits returned, he gave her a wicked grin, repeating her hashtag gesture with his fingers. "Hashtag Colm one, Ora zero."

She laughed, giving him the win. She could be generous. Considering she'd actually been the biggest winner.

"Get inside me, you lunatic." Kelli tried to draw him to her, but Colm resisted.

"Hang on. Let me grab a condom."

For a moment, Kelli was tempted to tell him to skip it, but she shoved that ridiculous thought away fast. She was jumbling up things that couldn't be jumbled.

The sex with Colm was great, but that was all it was. Sex.

That was all it could be because her plan remained the same. Her desire for a baby hadn't dimmed a single bit.

Colm retrieved the condom and slid it on.

She shoved away all thoughts of babies for now. Tonight wasn't about that.

"Come here," she whispered, crooking her finger at him.

Colm moved back over her body and placed his cock at her opening. They groaned in unison as he slid deep in one slow thrust.

"You feel so good," he said, holding his weight on his elbows so he could kiss her again.

He tilted his hips in an easy, gentle rhythm as he made love to her mouth.

God. It finally dawned on her why sex with Colm felt so different, so special.

With other men, it had always been fucking.

But Colm didn't do that. Instead, he made her feel cherished, precious. Important to him.

If this was his standard operating procedure, she couldn't understand how he'd remained single so long.

"Colm," she murmured, her hands stroking his back, her lips sliding over his bearded face.

"That's right, Kell. Say my name. Remember it's me." He lifted up, his weight on his hands as he increased his pace, taking her harder. Deeper. She lifted her hips each time he slid back in, needing more, demanding more, and he answered the call with more force, more pleasure.

It was as if she'd triggered something inside him when she spoke his name. And now, holy shit, he was staking a claim, imprinting his name on her body, in her memory.

"Colm. God! I'm..."

"I'm there too. Say my name, Kelli."

"Colm!" she cried, white light flashing behind her closed eyes.

"Dammit. Open your eyes and say my name!"

Kelli fought to give him what he wanted as he continued to slam inside her even harder. Her orgasm continued. She couldn't come down. She didn't fucking want to. Not ever.

"Colm. Colm. Colm..." His name became a chant as he held her gaze captive, his eyes never leaving hers, so that she saw it the second he was there too.

"Fuck. Kelli. God... *Kelli*," he breathed, her name almost a sigh as he came as well, his face etched with intense pleasure that almost looked like pain.

For several moments, neither of them moved or looked away. They simply lay there, connected, gasping for breath, staring.

Colm had been in her life since she was five years old. And tonight, it felt like she was seeing him for the very first time.

CHAPTER ELEVEN

Colm leaned back in his chair at Pat's Pub and rubbed his way-too-full stomach. Padraig sat across from him, doing the same thing. They were both suffering the aftereffects of Aunt Riley's Thanksgiving dinner.

"Every year, I say I'm not going to overeat," Colm murmured, closing his eyes as he fought off the desire to take a brief turkey-induced nap.

"Me too," Padraig said. "Then I see that homemade stuffing with the real bacon bits and I start shoving it in my face like it's my job."

"We haven't even had dessert yet."

Padraig groaned. "I'm going to explode if I eat Mom's pumpkin pie."

Colm cracked one eye open. "You skipping it?"

"Don't be insane. Of course not."

"Damn. Thought that meant there would be more for me."

Despite being closed, the noise level in the pub currently rivaled that of St. Patrick's Day when the place was filled to the rafters with the local patrons.

The Collins family had grown too large over the past few years to celebrate holidays together in someone's house, so they'd moved the festivities to the pub.

Pop Pop had always closed the pub on Thanksgiving, even though many other restaurants stayed open, claiming it was one of the best business days of the year.

Pop Pop insisted holidays were for family, not for making a buck. And since taking over the management of the pub and Sunday's Side, Colm's dad, Tris, Aunt Keira, and Uncle Ewan had kept up that same policy, closing so that the whole family could be together.

Looking around the room, Colm couldn't help but smile and feel blessed. Hunter and Uncle Sky were playing their guitars, a bunch of the little kids dancing around, laughing at the silly songs they were making up.

His mom and aunts were sitting around one large table, drinking wine, reminiscing about past holidays.

His dad and Pop Pop and uncles were sitting at the bar, watching football on the big screen, alternating between cheering or shouting at the refs.

They'd already done the eternal "say what you're thankful for" deal prior to eating the meal. As the family continued to grow, the time it took for everyone to have their turn to speak had expanded exponentially.

Pop Pop always started it, lifting a bottle of Jameson and demanding everyone's attention.

It usually took a few minutes to quiet the crowd, but

once everyone saw the Jameson, the conversations would end and they'd all turn to Pop Pop.

Pop Pop said the same thing every year. His grandfather was grateful for the roof over his head and the food in his belly, but most of all, he was thankful for the greatest family a man could ever ask for. Those words never failed to put a lump in Colm's throat.

Then Pop Pop would lift the bottle of whiskey, take a sip, and pass it on. After that, everyone took a turn, sharing what they were thankful for that year before drinking the whiskey.

Colm had said he was grateful for his thriving practice, for his mom and dad and brother. Like Pop Pop, he typically said the same thing every year as well. But this year, he made an addition...saying he was also very thankful for blackouts.

Then he took a drink of the whiskey and passed the bottle before anyone could question him on it, though he caught the knowing expression on Sunnie's face and the curious one on Padraig's.

Kelli admitted she'd told Sunnie, Darcy, and Yvonne about their blackout adventure on Halloween, and he'd gotten the sense she thought he'd be upset by that.

In truth, Colm had secretly been pleased that she wasn't trying to hide what they'd done. For some reason, it had given him hope that she would soon come to accept what he already knew. The curse had struck and there was no going back now.

He knew things weren't exactly clear sailing. Neither of them had brought up her desire for a baby, but Colm didn't believe for a minute Kelli had changed her mind. Nor should she.

The only thing he wanted to do was convince her to

reconsider whose baby she would be carrying. If she was on the same page as him...that would be simple. Because he was already planning their future together.

Kelli still hadn't caught up. Which meant he had his work cut out for him. And then some.

"You haven't been around much the past week. Work keeping you busy?" Padraig asked.

"Not really," Colm said. He'd actually been leaving work early and going over to Kelli's apartment after work every single day since Friendsgiving. At some point, he was going to have to figure out how to work a full day without succumbing to the need to be with her. As it was, his new normal consisted of hightailing it across town so that he was in the apartment and waiting for her when she got home from school.

Of course, given the way Kelli tackled him within two seconds of dropping her bag by the door, he'd say she was suffering the same unending, aching desire to be with him as well.

Padraig waited for him to explain, but Colm didn't.

"So," Padraig said. "Blackouts?"

Colm chuckled, surprised his twin had managed to hold that question in for so long.

"Blackouts," Colm repeated, adding nothing else. He liked to make his brother work for things.

And Padraig, bless him, always took the bait. "Care to elaborate."

Colm hadn't purposely kept Padraig in the dark about Kelli. The truth was, he simply hadn't had the opportunity to talk to him. But even as he considered that, he couldn't help but wonder how Padraig would respond. After all, it was Padraig who'd broken up all the fights between him and Kelli when they were growing up. "I slept with Kelli that night."

"My Kelli?"

Colm sighed. He really was going to have to break his brother of that habit. "*My* Kelli," he corrected.

Padraig didn't move or respond for a moment. Instead, he studied Colm's face hard, clearly searching to see if he was joking or telling the truth.

"I thought you were with Brooke that night," he said at last.

Colm grinned. "Hence my gratefulness for the blackout. *I* thought I was with Brooke, but it turned out to be Kelli."

"But Kelli knew she was with you?"

Colm shook his head. "She thought she was with Robbie. There was a bit of misunderstanding for about a week and a half, until we sorted it all out." Colm briefly recapped the story, including the part about Kelli thinking Colm was Padraig when she'd woken up to see him clean-shaven. His twin was laughing so hard by the end, he was wiping tears from his eyes.

"Holy crap. That might be the best story I've ever heard."

Colm agreed, not because of the humor—though it was pretty fucking funny—but because it had opened his eyes to the woman who'd been standing right in front of him for nearly thirty years. It was crazy to think he'd had to be blinded by a blackout before he could finally see clearly.

Once Padraig managed to pull himself together, more questions emerged.

"So, she's *your* Kelli now?" his brother asked.

Colm nodded. "Yeah. She doesn't realize it just yet, but she'll get there eventually."

"What does she think it is now?"

"Just sex."

Padraig choked on the sip of Guinness he'd just taken. "You're still sleeping together?"

"Oh yeah."

"And neither one of you has killed the other yet?"

Colm chuckled. "No. It's been...incredible. Perfect."

Padraig leaned closer. "Holy shit. You're in love with her!"

Colm didn't bother to deny it. He hadn't said the words to Kelli because she'd probably laugh him out of bed. This thing between them was brand-spanking new, something Kelli would point out to him, as if it was a valid argument. It wasn't. He didn't give a damn about the new car smell on them.

He'd fallen fast and hard. Done the exact same thing he'd always teased Padraig about.

"So...the curse?" Padraig asked, grinning widely.

Colm rolled his eyes and grimaced. "You know it's not a curse."

Padraig laughed loudly. "Wish I'd known all this before I'd said what I was thankful for because I'd like to change my answer now."

"Let me guess. You're thankful for getting to see me eat crow."

His brother shook his head. "Nope. Thankful that my two best friends in the world found each other. Kelli's always been like a sister to me, and now—"

Colm held up his hands to cut Padraig off. "Do me a

favor. Don't say the marriage word in front of Kelli yet. Don't even say the relationship word. She's..." Colm couldn't quite decide *what* she was. He knew she was at a definite cross-roads in her life. Before the two of them crash-landed into each other, she'd sworn off men and dating in order to focus on becoming a mother.

He'd seen the way she'd looked at Caitlyn on Halloween. Knew he was fighting an uphill battle.

"She's..." Padraig prompted.

His cell and Padraig's beeped at the same time. They glanced at their phones, and then at each other.

"She's outside," Colm said, standing up. "You get the wine. I'll get the door."

Padraig nodded and laughed. Kelli had just spent all day alone with her mother. While Colm looked forward to the holidays, Kelli did not, frequently referring to Thanksgiving and Christmas as her journeys to hell and back.

About a decade earlier, she'd started her own new Thanksgiving tradition, escaping her mother as soon as humanly possible, then joining the Collins family for dessert. And wine. A lot of wine.

He flipped the dead bolt on the front door of the pub, trying not to laugh at the haggard expression on her face.

"How's Barb?" he joked.

"Speak that name to me again and I *will* kill you."

He tugged her inside, locking the door again. Padraig was already on his way over to them, a large glass of merlot—and the bottle—in his hands.

"Paddy. My hero. You are the most wonderful man on the planet. Marry me."

Colm expected Padraig to give his standard response, to

claim she was too much woman for him, but instead, his brother said, "I'd love to, Kell, but it sounds like you're already taken."

Kelli turned to Colm. "Told him about Halloween, huh?"

"Sort of surprised *you* didn't tell me," Padraig said.

She shrugged. "Figured I'd leave that to Colm. I told Sunnie, Yvonne, and Darcy and didn't want to hog all the fun of seeing people's reactions when the bomb was dropped."

Padraig laughed. "So you really thought you and I..." He wiggled his eyebrows suggestively, letting her know that was his favorite part of the story.

"Don't remind me. That was a rough week and a half."

Padraig wrapped his arm around her shoulders. "You could've told me. I'm not as fragile as you and my brother choose to believe."

She gave Padraig a quick kiss on the cheek. "I know that. I'm sorry. Next time. Full disclosure."

"Not going to be a next time," Colm said, playfully knocking his brother's arm away from Kelli. "And hands off my girl. Drink up, Kelli. It'll make you feel better."

"Not sure a bottle's going to cut it this year," she said as she lifted the glass. "Nothing short of hooking up an IV of wine is going to help me forget the nightmare I just left."

Kelli took a long drink, chugging nearly half the glass. She was oblivious to the fact her arrival had been noticed by most of his family, and the room had gotten quiet.

When she finally lowered the glass, she looked around, confused, until the light went on. "Okay, okay. You got me. I've fallen off the wagon again. Who had Thanksgiving?"

Colm chuckled and raised his hand. "I did."

"Of course you did."

"Barb never lets me down."

Kelli rolled her eyes, though the wine was already working its magic. Her shoulders visibly relaxed as she lifted her glass. "Happy Thanksgiving," she called out to everyone. "This year, like every year, I'm grateful for the Collins family. And wine."

Everyone laughed as several of his cousins, as well as his parents, came over to say hello. Colm remained next to her, fighting the urge to pull her close and kiss her.

Once the crowd around them thinned out, he took the wineglass from her and placed it on a nearby table, then he grasped her hand and tugged her to the quiet corridor at the back of the pub that led to the restrooms and storage closet.

He wondered if she'd insist on playing it cool in front of his family, but he should have known better. The second he turned to face her, she was there, her hands in his hair, kissing him with an air of...desperation.

Colm gripped her waist, pulling her closer, until they were breast to chest. They weren't in the main pub area, but they weren't exactly hidden either. Anyone in his family could happen to peer down the corridor and see them.

Not that he gave a shit. He was ready to tell the world about the two of them.

Kelli moaned as his tongue touched hers, and she pulled away. "You taste *so* good."

"Aunt Riley puts on one heck of a Thanksgiving feast. I ate everything. Twice."

"Barb managed to outdo herself this year, too. I honestly didn't think she could find a way to make the turkey even drier. And she's on some stupid diet, so we didn't get real mashed potatoes. Only mashed cauliflower."

Colm winced. "Sacrilege."

"Right?"

There were tense lines around her eyes and mouth that only appeared after a day spent with her mother. Colm didn't like seeing them there.

He wrapped his arms around her, pulling her in for a hug, and he was thrilled when Kelli sank into it, her cheek pressed tightly to his chest, her arms adding their own strength to the embrace.

"I don't understand how someone can be that genuinely unhappy for sixty years," she murmured.

Colm had to agree. When he looked back over the years, he couldn't think of a single time he'd ever seen Barb with a smile that didn't look forced or faked, and he was fairly certain he'd never heard her laugh. Which made it even more incredible to him that Kelli had made it out with such an amazing sense of humor. She was quick to laugh and rarely without a smile. "Me either."

"Apparently, she was asked not to chair the fire station potluck this year. I know it's because she drove the rest of the committee nuts the last two years."

He chuckled. "Jeez, Kell. Only your mom could get fired from a volunteer position."

"I know. She was super pissed off and said the whole thing was going to go straight to hell without her running the show. Then she spent forty-five minutes bitching about something she'd heard through the grapevine about my dad. Apparently, a friend of a friend of a friend ran into him here in the city a few months ago."

"You didn't know he was in Baltimore?" Colm asked.

Kelli shook her head but didn't separate from the hug, still clinging. "Nope." There was precious little emotion behind that response, which simply reinforced the fact that Kelli had stopped expecting anything from the man a long time ago.

Kelli's parents had divorced when she was thirteen. Not that it came as a surprise to anyone—Kelli included—except Barb.

Kelli had actually confessed once she was shocked her dad had managed to stick around that long.

Barb, however, was blindsided by her husband's departure, and her general unpleasantness before that had turned to hardcore bitterness after. She criticized her ex to anyone who would listen and had for the past twenty-plus years. Time had not healed her wounds. Not even a little bit.

Mr. Peterson had tried to remain a part of Kelli's life the first few months after he'd left. Until his ex-wife made it too impossible. Then he moved across the country to Denver, met a woman with two sons, and remarried. As far as Colm knew, Kelli and her dad exchanged birthday cards and spoke on the phone a couple times a year. If she'd ever wanted more than that from her dad, she'd never expressed it.

Actually, after her dad split, Kelli had begun to turn to *his* father whenever she needed help with something she probably would have gone to Mr. Peterson for. It was Colm's dad, Tris, who taught her how to drive, throwing her in the car with him and Padraig, claiming it was just as easy to teach three teens as it was two. Dad had taught her how to change a tire, how to check the engine oil, how to fish. It was his dad whom Kelli had asked to go with her when she'd saved up enough money for her first piece-of-shit car.

Colm placed a soft kiss to the top of her head. "I'm sorry it was such a rough day, but hey, at least it's over."

"That would comfort me more if Christmas wasn't a month away. I'm considering running away with the gypsies."

"What if..." Colm took a deep breath, shocked by what he was about to offer, but he did it anyway. "What if you invite Barb to join all of us here for Christmas dinner? There are enough of us that if we all take a turn, no one should have to spend more than ten minutes with her."

Kelli lifted her head, her expression one of longing and horror.

Jesus. Only Kelli could pull off a look like that.

Then she leaned closer and sniffed his breath. "Have you been drinking?"

Colm narrowed his eyes. "No, Kell."

"Why would you subject your family to that?"

He chuckled. "They all know your mom. And just like you, they're fine with her. In small doses. We'll divide and conquer. What do you say?"

Kelli quietly studied his face for a full minute, obviously giving him time to come to his senses. He stared her down.

"I think that might be the nicest thing anyone has ever done for me."

He laughed loudly. "Shit. Talk about a low bar."

Kelli tilted her head. "Seriously?"

He revised his statement. "Okay, yeah. You're right. It's a damn high bar."

"Just the same," she said, "maybe you should clear it with your family. I really don't want to impose."

"It's not an imposition." Colm knew his family would be fine with it, especially when they found out about his and Kelli's change in relationship status.

Deep down, Colm was hoping this Christmas would be the first in a lifetime of holidays he and Kelli would spend together as a couple. And he knew perfectly well that meant Christmases with Barb as well.

Colm pressed his forehead against hers. "I guess you're going to make me go be social, aren't you? Or can I convince you to go upstairs for a quickie?"

"No quickie." She shook her head, though she was grinning widely. His invitation to Christmas seemed to have lifted the weight of the world off her shoulders. "I haven't had my pumpkin pie yet, and there's no way I'm taking a chance on missing it. You know how those vultures are once the desserts come out."

Kelli's favorite part of Thanksgiving was his mom's pumpkin pie. She loved it so much, Mom baked one for her for Christmas every year that, as her mom said, "Kelli doesn't have to share."

And Kelli didn't.

She didn't even slice the Christmas gift pie. Just grabbed a fork and went after it.

"Well, if you're not going to come up for the quickie, you're coming up to spend the night. Nonnegotiable."

Kelli gave him a kiss on the cheek. "I'm not a fool, Colm. I'm not about to fight you on something I want. Badly." She ran her hand down his chest suggestively before drifting even lower. She just barely grazed his covered cock, but it was enough to wake the boy up. "I'm thinking a blowjob might be on the books, thanks to the Christmas invite."

"Dammit," he muttered. "An erection and jeans don't mix, beauty. You know that."

She gave him a wicked grin and another stroke, leaving him rock-hard. "I do know that. That's what makes it so much fun for me."

"Payback's a bitch, Kell. Just remember."

She lifted one shoulder as if she didn't have a care in the world, then she turned back toward the dining area of the pub just as Aunt Riley yelled out, "Dessert!"

He heard Kelli laughing, perfectly aware she'd left him at a disadvantage as she disappeared among the crowd of his family, all of whom were jockeying for position around the cakes and pies.

Colm readjusted his pants, counted to twenty, then pictured Barb in a bikini. By the time he'd gotten himself under control and to the dessert line, the pumpkin pie was long gone. He looked over and spotted Kelli with a huge slice.

He narrowed his eyes because, well, it was his favorite too.

She lifted her hand and revealed two forks.

Oh yeah, Colm thought.

This was definitely love.

Now he just had to convince *her*.

CHAPTER TWELVE

"Well, look what the cat dragged in. Haven't seen you since Thanksgiving, lad. Come have a pint with me."

Colm grinned as Pop Pop waved him over. He'd been in court all day and he was running on fumes. He had actually just planned to swing by to pick up some more clothes, then head over to Kelli's.

But a pint with his grandfather was something he was never too busy to say no to.

His dad came out of the back and smiled when he saw him. "Hey, stranger. Where the hell have you been?"

Colm sank down on the stool next to Pop Pop. "Long day in court."

"That accounts for today, but you've been scarce since that Friendsgiving party you all throw every year. What's going on with you?" Dad asked.

Obviously, Padraig hadn't filled Dad and Pop Pop in on

Kelli. He'd have to remember to thank his twin. Kelli was right. It was fun to drop the bomb.

"Well..." he drawled, dragging out the word. It had the desired effect.

Pop Pop loved secrets, and he winked. "Oh yeah. Our boy's up to something."

Colm grinned wickedly. "You think so?"

Of course, Pop Pop, the astute man, had been around the night of karaoke. The night the light went on, so Colm suspected his grandfather already had a guess about what was coming. "Confession is good for the soul, Colm. Let's have it."

"You think I have something to confess?" he teased.

"Jesus. We don't have all day. The happy hour crowd is going to descend soon, Son. While I know the lawyer in you likes to plead the fifth—" Dad joked.

Colm grinned. "Neither confirm nor deny, Dad."

"Yeah. You made my life a living hell with that motto when you were a teenager. But I think you'll feel better if you just come out with it. Who is she?"

Colm laughed. "Kelli."

"Kelli who?" Dad asked, proving to Colm just how unlikely his feelings for the girl he'd known since he was five were.

Colm rolled his eyes. "*Kelli,*" he stressed.

"Paddy's Kelli?" It made sense that Dad considered Kelli Padraig's. The two of them had always been thick as thieves, while he and Kelli had solely existed in a *barely tolerant of each other* realm for most of their lives. Even so...he was getting damn tired of hearing her referred to as his brother's.

"Yeah."

Dad rubbed his chin, not bothering to conceal his surprise. "Huh. Well how 'bout that? Gotta admit, I didn't see that one coming."

Pop Pop clapped his hands together. "I can't tell you how happy this makes me, lad. That girl is the bee's knees."

Colm took a sip of the Guinness his father had just set down in front of him. "Yeah. She is." Then he looked at his dad. "And it took me by surprise too."

"When did this start up?" Dad asked.

"Halloween."

"Ahhhh." His father nodded. "And now I understand your gratefulness for blackouts. I'll have to tell your mom. She's been curious about it since Thanksgiving."

"Yeah. It's been a pretty awesome November. It's just..." Colm was happier than he'd been in a very long time, but even so, he was aware of the ax poised just over his head.

He needed advice, and he figured these two men were the perfect ones to give it to him. They'd both fought for and won the hearts of their true loves.

"You and Mom were friends before you fell in love, right?" Colm asked his dad.

Dad nodded. "Yeah. She was married to that abusive asshole, James, when she first started coming to the pub every Wednesday. We talked about everything under the sun. Then she got divorced and we fell in love, got married."

"You're forgetting she left for a year, Tris," Pop Pop added.

"I like to purposely forget that part, Pop. Killed me when she was gone. But I understand why she did it. She needed time to figure out how to stand on her own two feet."

"So you were in love with her before she left," Colm clarified.

"I'm Collins through and through, Colm. Which means I fell fast and hard and forever...way before she left. But you know all this. Why the questions?"

Pop Pop stared him down. "For a man who considers love a curse, your interest seems odd. Unless..."

"Unless?"

Pop Pop didn't push. Instead, he said, "I think it's time for you to explain the *it's just* part of your previous comment. What's going on, lad?"

"Kelli has set something in motion as far as her future is concerned. Something she planned to do alone. Which means the timing on starting a relationship is...not great."

Dad frowned. "That's vague as hell."

"Her clock is ticking," Colm said. "She's sworn off the dating scene and made the decision to become a mother. On her own."

"I see," Dad said. "I have to admit that doesn't surprise me. Kelli's never had much luck in love, though I can't figure out what's wrong with the single men in this city. She's definitely a catch."

"She doesn't suffer fools gladly," Colm said.

Dad chuckled. "That's true. She doesn't. She also doesn't make rash decisions, so if she's decided she can handle being a mother on her own, she can."

"Tell us the rest of it, lad."

Pop Pop really didn't need Colm to say the words. He already knew what he was going to say. But the old guy was canny, which meant he also knew Colm needed to come clean about everything.

"I'm in love with her."

Dad blew out a long breath. "Damn. I was starting to worry we'd never see the day. You've changed girlfriends more than most people change underwear."

"Very funny," Colm replied, eyes narrowed, though there was no heat behind the phrase. "I think she's the one."

Pop Pop studied his face. "You don't think, Colm. You know."

"Yeah. I *do* know. But like I said, the timing on this...is tricky."

"This isn't a new relationship, Colm. I venture to guess you know Kelli better than any woman you've ever dated," Dad said.

"I already know all the stuff about her that's going to drive me crazy, and she knows the same about me."

Dad laughed. "Well, that's one way to look at it."

"So you're right. This isn't the beginning, but...Kelli doesn't consider this a beginning to *anything*. She thinks we're just—" Colm stopped when he remembered who he was talking to.

Pop Pop winked at him. "Your father and I have been around long enough to fill in the rest of that statement. So am I to understand you haven't spoken to her about wanting a commitment? A relationship?"

Colm shrugged. "It's only been a couple of weeks, and given the fact she's just sworn off men...that she's seriously pursuing this single motherhood thing..."

"Let's break it into pieces. She wants children, Colm," Pop Pop said. "That desire isn't going to go away. Having kids is a huge step, one that Kelli is obviously ready to take. What about you?"

"I want kids." As soon as Colm said it, he realized he probably wanted them every bit as much as Kelli. "I've always wanted kids."

"You'll be a great father, lad," Pop Pop said, gripping his shoulder. "At heart, you're as peaceful and gentle as a dove. Wonderful attributes for a man with children."

"Shit. You found a way to make me hate the meaning of my name less. How long have you been holding on to that gem?"

Pop Pop winked, even as he jokingly said, "Language."

Colm smiled appreciatively at his grandfather, touched by his genuine belief in him. "If I could be half the father you and Dad were, I'd be happy. Not sure how either one of you did it."

Pop Pop had lost Grandma Sunday when all of his kids were still living at home, Aunt Keira—the oldest, only eighteen at the time—all the way down to Uncle Sean, who'd still been in elementary school. Somehow he'd managed to run the pub and raise their seven kids on his own.

Pop Pop chuckled. "Well, I'm not going to say it was all sunshine and roses. God knows Riley and Sean tested me at times."

Colm glanced at his dad, grinning. "And I know Paddy was a handful."

Dad laughed. "Yeah. Paddy. Let's go with that. So, you've been dating Kelli for a couple of weeks. That's early in any relationship to be thinking about kids."

"I know, but..." Colm didn't want to say what he was really thinking because he figured he'd sound like an idiot. Two weeks *was* too early.

"But it hasn't been two weeks," Pop Pop finished for him. "Not really."

"Seem to recall having a similar conversation like this with Paddy," Dad added. "The day after he met Mia."

Colm took a swig of beer, hoping it would dislodge the lump in his throat. "He was ready to marry her that day."

"He was. And he and Mia had only known each other hours. Pop and I told him to slow his roll, to take some time to get to know her. I'm not sure..."

"Not sure?" Colm prodded.

His dad shrugged. "Hindsight is twenty-twenty. I probably would say the same thing to him today, but the fact remains, Paddy was right. He knew she was meant to be his."

"Kelli and I have known each other a long time. A lifetime."

"The heart knows what the heart wants, Colm. My heart beat for Lane from the first second she sat down at the end of this bar and we started talking. And my feelings for her continued to grow. They're *still* growing. Every day I look at her and can't believe she's mine. That she can still spend year after year with this grumpy, opinionated, getting-bigger-around-the-middle old man."

"You finally realized you and Kelli are both walking in the same direction. That you have the same hopes and desires." Pop Pop had described his relationship with Grandma Sunday that way once. Said that love had snuck up on him, one look, one word, and then...

"Click," Colm whispered, recalling that conversation so many years ago.

Pop Pop smiled widely. "Just like *Romeo and Juliet*. But with a better ending."

"So I'm not crazy?" Colm asked.

"No, lad." Pop Pop squeezed his shoulder. "You're just in love. And it's about damn time."

Colm laughed. "Language, Pop Pop."

CHAPTER THIRTEEN

Kelli sat on her couch, staring at the TV like a zombie. The damn thing wasn't even on, but she didn't have the energy to lean forward to pick up the remote. Mojo was curled next to her, purring away, happy to have her home from work.

Kindergartners in the month of December, hopped up on Santa Claus and candy canes, were a blight on the planet. There were only two more school days until holiday break and she was *not* going to make it.

Her phone pinged, and she groaned. It was on the coffee table next to the remote. She considered ignoring it, until it pinged again.

She forced herself forward, reaching for the phone and the remote at the same time. Work smarter, not harder. Then she fell back against the couch once more.

She glanced at the screen and smiled. Then she caught herself.

She was smiling at a goddamn text from Colm Collins.

Padraig would tease her endlessly after her years of bitching about Colm if he could see her now.

Did you eat yet?

Colm didn't even bother to wait for a reply before texting again.

On my way. Stopping for takeout.

He was bringing food.

Right to her house.

There were a lot of past sins she could forgive him for, simply for feeding her. The Barbie doll haircut in kindergarten; the Smelly Kelli nickname; telling the entire fourth grade class she had lice when she didn't; stealing her clothes one night senior year when she was skinny-dipping in a friend's pool, so she'd had to drive home wrapped in just a towel.

Maybe she *didn't* forgive him for that one. Her mother had been awake when she got home and still brought up "the naked incident" whenever she wanted to make a point about Kelli being too wild and needing to settle down.

She texted him back.

Need wine too.

She could almost imagine him chuckling.

Bottle enough or should I go for a case?

Okay. He was forgiven for the naked incident too.

The man knew her well. Very well. That was proving to be very helpful. Endearing, even.

Is that a rhetorical question? It's Monday.

She half expected him to throw in her face the fact there were only two more days in the workweek before holiday break, but the wise man held his piece.

Kelli glanced around the room and considered tidying up

a bit. It was a brief lapse she recovered from quickly. Instead, she turned on the TV to watch the episode of "Ellen" she'd recorded.

Colm let himself in just as the show ended. He'd always had a key to her place—or, she should say, she'd always kept an extra key at the Collins Dorm in case she ever locked herself out. She wasn't sure exactly when Colm had taken it from the tiny dish of "extra" keys that resided on a small table in their living room and added it to his keyring, but since it meant she didn't have to get up and let him in, she was cool with it.

Mojo hopped up from the couch instantly, rubbing around Colm's ankles. He'd stolen her cat, the fickle feline perfectly content with Kelli until Colm showed up. Then it was like Kelli was invisible.

His arms were laden down with Chinese take-out boxes, and she laughed when she saw him carrying an honest-to-God case of wine.

She placed her hand on her heart. "Colm. My hero."

He tilted his head and stared at her for a second like he was waiting for something.

"What?" she asked.

"Paddy gets a marriage proposal and all he ever does is bring you a *glass* of wine. I'm carrying a case here, Kell. And juggling takeout."

She rolled her eyes. "Fine. I'll let you go down on me after dinner."

"You're a cruel, cruel woman."

"I've been called worse."

Colm carried the food and the wine into the kitchen, Mojo hot on his heels. He bent down to pick up her cat, rubbing behind Mojo's ears, cooing ridiculous—but sweet—words to the tiny creature.

"Who's a good kitty? Who's the sweetest kitty in the world?" Mojo rubbed her nose against Colm's cheek, as big a fan of his beard as Kelli was.

He put Mojo down, opening a can of cat food to put in her bowl.

Kelli considered standing up to help him dish their dinner out and pour the wine, but her body was rejecting all thoughts of movement. It really had been the day from hell. Usually she had more energy, but today had zapped every ounce of it.

He returned to the living room with two glasses of wine, setting them down on the coffee table. "Damn. You really *did* have a rough day."

"Look that good, do I? Personally, I blame the fucking Elf on the Shelf."

He grinned, though clearly confused. "Why's that?"

"Parents put those things out in December with the threat that Santa has eyes and ears everywhere in the home. So the little bastards get their shitty behavior out with *me* so they can look like angels at home. Next year, I'm putting an elf on the freaking bookshelf in the classroom in September and telling them *my* elf is the Head Elf and his word is law with Santa."

"A dastardly plan. I like it."

"Plus, today was the holiday open house, so all the parents showed up," she called out as Colm returned to the kitchen. The two rooms were connected with an open island separating them, so she could still see him, still talk to him as he rummaged around for plates, forks, and napkins.

"Do you know how exhausting it is to smile and be pleasant all fucking day?"

Colm was grinning when he returned with the food. Rather than claim one of the empty chairs, he plopped down right next to her on the couch, bending forward to give her a quick kiss.

"It sounds absolutely terrible," he said, commiserating just enough that she knew he was half serious, half teasing. Which for her was actually the right mix.

Somewhere along the line, they'd fallen into a nightly routine where they ate dinner together in the living room after work, watching the local news or some repeat of a sitcom, like they were an old couple who'd been married for a hundred years. Then, they either went for a walk along the waterfront or to the pub or...more often, straight to her bedroom, where they spent hours tangled up together doing the naked mambo before falling asleep, only to wake up the next morning for a rinse and repeat of the previous day.

Kelli would have thought such an existence would bore her by now, but the truth was, she loved it. Loved not eating and sleeping alone. Loved having someone to bitch about her day with. Loved listening to him gripe and groan about his.

"Two more days. Just two more days," she said, picking up the plate of sesame chicken he'd dished out for her. "And then I'm free for two whole weeks."

"Yeah. You are." Colm started eating his Mongolian beef, falling uncharacteristically quiet. Typically, he was talking her ear off about work or his current case or sharing the latest in Caitlyn's morning sickness saga. The poor woman couldn't hold anything down until early afternoon. According to Colm, his cousin had discovered a completely new shade of green whenever he described Caitlyn's complexion just before her mad dash to the office bathroom.

But today...nothing.

"You okay?" she asked, putting her plate down when it became obvious something was bothering him. He wasn't looking at her, but he wasn't watching TV either. Instead, he seemed very deep in thought.

Colm sighed. "What are we doing, Kell?"

"Eating Chinese?"

He gave her a "really?" look that confused her even more than his question.

"What do you mean?"

"What is this? Between us?"

Shit. She was suddenly sorry she'd asked. It was easy to just roll with whatever this was as long as they didn't discuss it, or define it.

She'd sworn off men and dating back in October, and at the time, she'd meant that vow with every fiber of her being. She was tired of trying to find Mr. Right in a sea of Mr. Mehs.

Then Halloween.

Then the blackout.

Then Colm.

Since then, she'd switched onto autopilot, riding this wave as long as she could, even though she knew that eventually it would crash into the shore.

Looked like they'd just faceplanted into the sand.

"Colm...I don't." She swallowed heavily, not wanting to say the rest. She cleared her throat and dug deep for them. "I don't think there can be an us."

"I beg to differ."

Colm was a lawyer. Which meant this conversation wasn't going to end easily. And, of course, he'd hit her with this on a day when she was weary straight to the bone after a freaking exhausting day at work.

"Do we really have to talk about this now?"

"Yeah. We do. Because we're out of time. Holiday break is here."

She blinked, trying to figure out why he'd drawn that line in the sand...

And then she realized he hadn't. *She* had. Her plans with Robbie had.

Although God only knew if those were still in effect. She didn't have a clue if things between him and Brooke had stuck. If they had...well, she knew from her point of view, she wouldn't like the idea of her new boyfriend donating sperm to an ex, no matter how innocent and platonic it was.

"I told you before this started that I was taking myself off the market."

"We're dating, Kelli."

"No, we're not. We're having sex." She was the queen of contrary, and she knew it. She wasn't proud of it at the moment, but years of bickering with Colm had her working on instinct, used to saying white every single time he said black, right or not.

Colm rolled his eyes. "I've spent every night here for the last two weeks. I have two suits hanging in your closet, a toothbrush in your bathroom, at least three pairs of dirty socks strewn around this living room floor, and my beer is in your fridge. We *are* dating."

She narrowed her eyes. "You insidious bastard." There was no heat behind her words. In fact, her tone probably told him she knew exactly what they were doing. She just didn't want to admit it.

"Every time I swing by the apartment for a change of clothes, some member of my family makes sure to ask how my girlfriend is." Apparently, Colm wasn't finished making his case. Typical.

She sighed. "I shouldn't have let things go this far."

Colm reached for her hand. "I know what you want, sweetheart. I know you're worried about losing more time, time you need to get what you want, but can't you give us just a little bit more?"

"How much more, Colm? My chances of conceiving after my next birthday go down to something like twelve percent. Plus, the risk of birth defects and miscarriages increase. I don't *have* more time."

They hadn't talked about her desire to have a baby since Halloween. He'd mentioned it briefly after the football game a few weeks earlier, but she'd dismissed it out of hand. After that, they just let themselves fall into this relationship— keeping it all surface-y, easy, only paying attention to the fun stuff, while pushing reality away.

He reached out and took her hand, giving it a gentle squeeze. "I get it."

She shook her head. "No. I don't think you do. I was an only child, Colm, and it sucked. I always wanted what you and Paddy had. A sibling, someone to play with, fight with. This isn't going to be a one-time thing for me. I need enough time..."

"To do it twice."

She smiled sadly. "A family of my own. I want it so badly. I ache for it. And I'm not going to be an overbearing mom, like mine is. My kids are going to pick out their own clothes when they're little, even if they don't match. They can put all those ridiculous colors in their hair in high school. I'm not putting up a stupid daily chore chart or badgering their poor teachers when they don't get the lead in the play or an A on an essay or—"

Colm tugged on her hand, pulling her close enough that he could wrap his arm around her shoulder and place a kiss on top of her head. "You're going to be an awesome mom. And I know Barb was a bit much..."

Kelli lifted her head and narrowed her eyes. "A bit?"

"But you realize all that overprotectiveness was done out of love, right?"

"Of course I do."

"Although I do think you're right to dial it all back a notch or thirty. Remember that time she made Miss Rivers cry when you didn't get the solo in 'Time to Say Goodbye' in our choral concert?"

"Oh my God. Poor Miss Rivers. I felt so bad for her."

She and Colm laughed at the memory.

Colm sobered up first. "So, more time is out of the question."

He hadn't posed that like a question, but she nodded just the same.

"Fine. Call Robbie and tell him no thanks. We'll stop using the condoms and—"

"Oh my God, no. Please stop right there, Colm. I can't... we can't..."

It was never a great idea to tell Colm he couldn't do something, and she realized her mistake the second she saw the set of his jaw. He was stubborn and tenacious when he got something in his head. It was why he was a great lawyer.

She needed to cut him off at the pass. "Think about it," she continued quickly. "We're at the beginning of this..."

"Relationship," he supplied.

She might not want to say it, but that didn't change what it was.

"Fine. Relationship," she conceded. "This is the honeymoon phase. All lust and fun. You and I have both been here about a million times."

"No, we haven't."

She considered that. Considered the last few weeks with Colm. He was right again. Neither of them had ever gotten quite this far. Their past relationships had never moved from dating and the occasional overnights to instant shacking up, which was definitely what this felt like.

"Okay," she said, trying to find her next argument. "Regardless of that, we both know lust fades. And the next phase is the one where someone walks away."

"I'm not walking away, Kelli."

"Everyone walks away, Colm."

"Is that what you really think?"

Was it? Kelli didn't know how to respond to that because until those words flew from her lips, so certain, so...

Oh God.

Bitter.

She'd sounded *bitter*.

A few thousand concrete bricks came crashing down on her head as she struggled to catch her breath, to think of some joke, some way to shove off the crushing weight on her chest before she suffocated.

It took a minute before she found her voice again. "I just don't think it's a good idea for you and I to..." Her words faded to nothingness...because she didn't know what else to say.

She wasn't sure what Colm saw in her face, but given how well he knew her, she figured he could tell she was silently freaking out.

And because he was a good man, he dropped that argument. Sort of.

"So use me as the sperm donor. Pretend I'm the orthodontist in Iowa."

"You want to gift me with sperm?" she asked incredulously.

"Why not?"

"You know why not. Colm, I didn't ask you originally for the same reason I didn't ask Paddy. Neither one of you would ever walk away from a kid you helped create. Besides, we don't live six states apart. We see each other. All. The. Time. You're going to see my baby a lot because I want your family to be a part of his or her life."

"You keep talking about this relationship like it's already over. Like we're going to erase the last month, rewind the clock, and go back to bickering and giving each other a hard time."

"If we were smart, that's exactly what we'd do."

She didn't miss the disappointment in his tone when he said, "You know better than that, Kell."

He was right. She did.

"We're not those people anymore. We couldn't be those two again if we tried."

"Colm—" she started.

"This is the new normal, Kelli. This. Right here. Right now."

She shook her head, searching desperately for some way to counter his claim, to prove him wrong, but she couldn't come up with a single thing. Which scared her even more.

Why was her gut telling her this wouldn't work? Was she really that jaded? That convinced forever didn't exist?

"Why are you shaking your head?" he asked. "What part of this is so hard for you to accept?"

Kelli wasn't sure if she was shaking her head at him or at herself, suddenly not liking all the hard facts hidden in shadow he was thrusting out into broad daylight. "Dammit, Colm. It's only been a month. That's way too soon to—"

"To what?" Colm interjected, rising from the couch. He was frustrated, and that emotion, suddenly wafting off him in waves, fueled her own aggravation. She stood too, refusing to give him the power position. They were standing toe-to-toe, facing each other down.

This stance, between them, was as familiar to her as breathing.

Colm waved his hands in the air. "Why do we need months or years to know what this is? Jesus, Kell! You *know* me. You know every fucking thing there *is* to know about me."

"You're not being practical," she countered.

"No. You're not thinking."

She narrowed her eyes, but before she could call him to task, he continued.

"What don't you know about me that you think is suddenly going to change this thing between us? Have you seen me in a bad mood in the past?"

"Of course I have. You were a complete pain in the ass all through puberty."

"Are my bad moods going to be a deal-breaker for you?"

"No. Of course not, but—"

"What about my temper?"

"What about it?" she asked.

"Is it too much? Do I ever scare you?"

She scowled. "Don't be ridiculous. Of course not. I have a way bigger temper."

He nodded. "You're right. You do. And it's not a deal-breaker for *me*. What about work? Do you think I'm a workaholic?"

"You work long hours sometimes, but no. You're not a workaholic."

"So my job isn't a problem for you?"

"No, but—"

"I'd ask you if you had any concerns about us in the bedroom, but we both know I'm more than capable of giving you mind-blowing orgasms every single night."

The old Kelli was digging deep for some way to wipe the cocky grin off Colm's face, but the asshole was right. *Again.* Sex was never going to be an issue for them. Unless it was the fact neither of them seemed capable of getting enough.

"Do you think I'd be a good father?"

His question knocked the breath from her—because it wasn't even something that required thought. "You'd be...an amazing father."

He'd been gathering a pretty good head of steam until that response. Her answer seemed to calm him down a bit, and he smiled. A charming, sweet, wonderful smile.

"What don't you know about me, Kelli, that you haven't learned in the last thirty years?"

The answer was simple.

Nothing.

And yet, she couldn't give it to him. Couldn't admit it.

"Can I...can you...give me some time?" Kelli couldn't think with him standing so closely. And she desperately needed time to gather her thoughts, to come to grips with some issues—that bitterness; that unexplored fear of Colm leaving her just as her father had, which she hadn't realized was there—before she gave him an answer.

Colm studied her face for a moment, then nodded. "Sure. What do you need? Five? Ten minutes?"

She laughed, loudly, leaning forward until her forehead was pressed against his chest. "God, you're a cocky son of a bitch," she said, between giggles. "A pain in the ass. A thorn in my side."

Colm wrapped his arms around her, his cheek pressed to the top of her head, swaying gently, until she managed to contain her mirth.

"I just need a little bit of time."

He sighed, the sound letting her know he didn't want to give it to her.

But...she *did* know him. Knew him well enough to know he'd give it to her anyway.

"Okay," he said at last. "But I'm telling you right now. I'm not staying away for long."

"I know that. I'll call you very soon. Honest."

He cupped her cheeks and kissed her, and she marveled over how he could pack so much into just one kiss.

One kiss.

Pleading.

Passion.

Possession.

And a promise that he was coming back.

Soon.

CHAPTER FOURTEEN

Colm returned to the pub...begrudgingly.

He'd put up a hell of a fight back at Kelli's, and she'd still asked for more time. He'd had the last two weeks to prepare his case, to come up with what he'd considered an ironclad argument. He knew Kelli's only defense would be the fact they'd only been a couple less than a month.

So he'd started a list of all the ways he could counter that argument. And he sort of thought he'd nailed it.

Until she'd looked at him with those sad, scared blue eyes and asked him for time to think.

He'd always thought himself made of pretty stern stuff, able to stand firm when he knew he was right, but dammit if she hadn't slayed him with one look.

She could have asked him to build a space shuttle and fly her to the moon with those eyes, and fuck him if he wouldn't be googling for a way to buy rocket fuel right now.

"What are you doing here?" Padraig asked as he dropped down onto a stool at the bar.

"I live here."

Padraig didn't respond to the sarcasm. Instead, he poured Colm a pint of Guinness and slid it in front of him.

His twin waited until Colm took a long swig, sucking down nearly half the beer, before he started the questioning. "What did you do?"

"Why do you assume I'm the one who fucked up?"

Padraig grinned. "I don't assume anything. It's you and Kelli. I had a fifty-fifty shot either way."

"I told her we were dating."

Padraig gave him a funny look. "She didn't know that?"

Colm grimaced. "It's Kelli. She didn't *want* to know that. Even though she did."

It spoke to the level of Padraig and Kelli's friendship that he not only understood that ridiculous statement but found it amusing. "That's my Kell. She'll always go down swinging."

Colm narrowed his eyes. "Thought we'd already determined she was *my* Kelli."

Emmy, who was sitting at the end of the bar, tapping away on her keyboard, paused and looked up at that. The woman was a master eavesdropper, though Colm could never quite figure out how she could write and listen to all the conversations happening at the pub at the same time.

Colm caught her eye. "She's *my* Kelli," he repeated for her benefit, feeling the need to stress that point to anyone and everyone.

Emmy just nodded and smiled and started typing again.

"So clue me in, Bro," Padraig said, leaning on the counter. "I thought things between you and Kelli were good. Why would she be so resistant to the concept of dating you?"

"You know about her baby plans." Kelli had pulled Padraig away after dessert at Thanksgiving, the two of them finally talking for ages about her hopes for the future and what she'd planned to do.

Padraig nodded. "She still planning to keep the sperm donor? And the timeline?"

Colm sighed. "Yeah. I told her it was time for us to figure some shit out since she's set this damn holiday break as go time."

"Did you ask for more time?"

Colm shook his head. "At first. But I knew she wouldn't go for it. So I asked to be the father."

"Wow." Padraig's amazement didn't really match the huge-ass grin on his face. "Talk about taking an abrupt left turn. Weren't you the guy who wasn't tying himself down to just one woman until he was at least forty?"

"You and I both know that was me talking out my ass. Trying to make myself feel better because love was eluding me."

"And Kelli rejected your offer?"

Colm shrugged. "Yeah. At first. Then..."

"Let me guess, you went full lawyer on her ass and started wearing her down with all your arguments."

Colm leaned back in his chair, scowling. "I simply reminded her that there was precious little she didn't know about me. I don't know why she thinks we need any more time to," Colm finger-quoted, "'get to know each other.'

Jesus. We've known each other our whole lives. What else is there to learn?"

Padraig lifted his hands in surrender as Colm became more impassioned with each word. "Hey, Bro. Listen. I'm on your side. I think you and Kelli are perfect for each other. But the truth is she's stubborn and headstrong, and once she's made up her mind about something, it's hard for her to back away from it. She's had this single-mom plan swimming around in her brain for the better part of a year. She's made the lists, the plans, studied the pros and cons. Then, the second she takes the leap and sets things in motion, you crawl in bed with her in the middle of a blackout and boom! Everything is tossed on its ear."

"I'm not trying to talk her out of having a baby. I just want it to be *our* baby." Colm finished his Guinness.

Padraig refilled it. "The thing is...Kelli is always waiting for the other shoe to drop."

Colm recognized the truth in that statement. Especially when he recalled her comment that everyone leaves eventually.

He considered those words from her perspective because he'd never heard her say anything with such outright assurance, and such...pain.

That was when he realized it wasn't *everyone* who had always walked away from her.

It was just one person.

Her dad hadn't just left her mom. He'd left Kelli. The asshole had been in town a few months ago and hadn't even bothered to call his daughter.

Colm had assumed that didn't bother her because she'd

never let on that it did. But he could see now that her pride wouldn't let her reveal her feelings about the matter.

Her dad's departure had hurt her, and he wasn't sure Kelli had ever faced up to it.

"I'm not her dad," Colm said. "I wouldn't leave her. Wouldn't leave our kids."

"And I'm sure Kelli knows that. Deep down inside. But she's had precious little luck with love, so I have no doubt you dropped those three little words on her and she freaked out."

Colm froze. "Shit," he muttered.

Padraig frowned. "Wait—you said them, right?"

Colm shook his head. "No. I...fuck...I said everything else."

Emmy stopped typing and looked straight at him, one eyebrow raised in disbelief. "You did all that arguing for a relationship and babies and you didn't tell her you loved her?"

"I should have told her," Colm moaned, realizing he'd dropped the ball in closing arguments.

"Dude," Padraig said. "You should have *led* with that."

Emmy sighed. "Rookie mistake."

Colm ran his hand through his hair. "I'm an idiot."

"So tell her," Padraig said.

Colm nodded, then glanced at Emmy. She was a romance writer, though she'd never told any of them her pen name. Not even Padraig, who was chomping at the bit to read one of her books.

"She asked for time to think, but she doesn't have all the facts. So...I should go back tonight, right?"

"What do *you* think?" Emmy asked.

"I'm going back."

She laughed softly. "Good call. I think it's safe to say you've hit the point in this romance where the hero tells the heroine he loves her, and they live happily ever after."

"Oh damn. Yeah. This is an important turning point. So set me up with a plot. Are you a fan of a big gesture?"

Emmy rolled her eyes. "No. I'm a fan of the words. Just go, you big fool."

Colm stood, walking to the end of the bar to give her a hug. "Thanks for the advice."

He didn't miss the tiniest glimmer in Padraig's eyes—jealousy?—as he did so.

"Good luck," Padraig called out as Colm headed back out the door he'd only entered twenty minutes earlier.

KELLI HAD RETURNED to the couch two seconds after Colm left, wishing she could channel her previous zombie state. That was an easier state of mind than her present one.

Too many things were bombarding her.

She hadn't realized how much her dad's departure had bothered until her argument with Colm. She'd been pissed off ever since learning he'd been in Baltimore recently and he hadn't visited, hadn't called to see if she wanted to do something with him. She would have met him for a lousy ten-minute chat over a cup of coffee...if he'd asked.

But he hadn't. And as much as it bugged her to admit it, that hurt.

Kelli leaned her head back. She really thought she'd gotten to a point where her parents couldn't hurt her anymore. Annoy her? Yes. Embarrass her? Absolutely. But hurt her? No.

She was suddenly awash in feelings she had no clue how to deal with—and it occurred to her that what she *really* wanted was to talk to Colm about it.

Colm. Who wanted a relationship with her. A long-term, let's-make-babies relationship.

No one had ever wanted that with her.

Like, no one.

Ever.

She'd dated so many here-one-day-gone-the-next guys, she hadn't even known how to respond to Colm's suggestion. Because it had taken her slightly off guard and surprised her. Even when it shouldn't have.

"God, I'm the world's biggest idiot," she muttered.

Mojo, who'd been curled up in a ball in her lap, glanced up as she spoke, then promptly went right back to sleep.

Colm said she knew him...and he was right. She did.

Which meant she knew he was perfect for her.

Colm Collins, her lifelong frenemy, was the man of her dreams. And instead of telling him that, she'd been a complete tool and told him she needed time.

Time for what?

She picked up Mojo, placing her on the cushion next to her and standing up, looking around the living room for her shoes. She was going over to the pub and she was going to—

She heard a key in the door of her apartment and immediately fought to school her features, to hide the smile fighting to erupt.

Colm was here. He'd come back.

He stepped inside, pausing when he found her standing there.

"Jesus, Colm. It hasn't even been an hour," she joked, so happy it was taking everything she had not to run across the room and leap into his arms.

She expected him to smile, but he didn't. In fact, he looked far too serious.

Shit. Had she screwed things up by asking for time? Had she hurt his feelings by rebuffing him?

"Colm—" She started to apologize, anxious to set things straight as quickly as possible.

He raised his hand to cut her off. "No. Wait. I had to come back because I realized there *was* something you don't know about me. Something I didn't tell you."

Oh God. Here it was. She should have known better, should have realized this was all too good to be true. She'd pushed Colm away and he'd wised up already, discovered a reason why this wouldn't work.

Her heart thudded painfully in her chest. If he told her he didn't want to see her anymore, she wasn't sure she could take it. She'd thought her heart had been broken a few times over the years, but she knew now her heart had never even been bruised.

"What is it?" she asked, hating how thin her voice was, how panicked she sounded.

Colm walked over to her, grasping her hands in his. "I..." She watched as he took a deep breath. "I'm going to say something to you that, well, I might have said it to other women in the past, but...I realize now I lied."

"Okay," she whispered.

"I love you, Kelli."

She gasped, but he wasn't finished.

"No. It's more than that. I'm in love with you. Completely, ridiculously, aggressively, *obnoxiously* in love with you."

Her heart, which had previously been thudding so hard she'd had trouble hearing, suddenly stopped beating. "Obnoxiously?"

He nodded. "It would appear...you're my curse."

She laughed. "You know, if any other man said that to me, I'd kick him out on his ass. But..." Her words got wobbly, and she felt tears forming in her eyes. "But with you...God. I'm your curse," she said, repeating the words she simply couldn't believe.

He stepped closer to her, reaching up to cup her face, to wipe away the tears with his thumbs. "Kelli," he whispered.

"I'm obnoxiously in love with you too."

He kissed her, a hard, long, lots-of-tongue kiss.

When they parted, she grinned. "Guinness."

"Paddy and Emmy spotted the flaw in my previous arguments. Said I left out the most important part."

"They were right."

"Well," Colm said, turning toward the door. "I know you need time, so I guess I'll just—"

She laughed. "Colm?"

"Yeah," he said, glancing over his shoulder at her with a wicked gleam in his eye.

"I was on my way to the pub."

"You were?" Kelli wasn't sure when his cocky, know-it-all grin had become a turn-on, but damn if she didn't go wet at the sight of it.

"Yeah. I don't need time. At all."

Colm crossed his arms. Bastard was going to make her work for it. "No? You sure?"

"Colm."

"What?"

"My bedroom. Now."

CHAPTER FIFTEEN

C olm grasped her hand and tugged her down the hallway. Mojo was hot on their heels, running ahead to jump on the bed when they entered Kelli's room.

Colm chuckled. "Not this time, sweet girl," he said, putting the cat back on the floor. Kelli's cat liked to cuddle in between them each night after they went to sleep, he and Kelli jokingly knocking the other's hand away when they petted her as she purred, fighting to be the favorite.

He turned back to Kelli, who was already unzipping her pants and pushing them and her panties down.

"Maybe you should leave that sweater on. It's hot."

Kelli rolled her eyes. "You got a thing for gingerbread?"

Colm wiggled his eyebrows suggestively. Kelli owned a seemingly endless collection of cutesy sweaters, which was apparently Wardrobe 101 for elementary school teachers. The current holiday-themed one was adorned by gingerbread men and said, "My kindergartners are SMART COOKIES."

"Nope. Just kindergarten teachers. They're surprisingly kinky in bed."

"You lucky bastard. Take off that suit and tie. You're not fooling anybody with that buttoned-up conservative look."

Colm loosened the knot in his tie, then pulled it free from the collar of his shirt. He wrapped it around his hand, fisting the silk. "Maybe I should hold on to this for later."

"Fancy a little bondage? I don't mind strapping you down and having my wicked way with you."

He chuckled. "I think we both know who's going to be on top, Kell."

She tilted her head playfully. "Do we? Because I'm not sure *you* do."

Colm stepped close to her and tugged her sweater over her head. Then he reached around her back and unhooked her bra with one quick flick. He looked down at her breasts and grinned. "God, I love your tits."

Kelli slapped his cheek lightly. "Sweet talker. Take off your pants."

"What about my shirt?"

"That's not holding me back from what I really want."

Colm shook his head as if disappointed. "I knew it. I'm just another sex toy, aren't I?"

Kelli laughed, tapping her fingertips together like the worst of the world's evil masterminds. "With you, my collection is complete," she said darkly.

Colm stripped off his shirt and pants in record time, gripping her waist to twist and then toss her onto the bed.

"Open those legs and submit to me, woman," he said in true caveman tone.

Kelli giggled, but it wasn't lost on him that she scooted to the center of the bed and then obeyed.

Colm lost no time crawling over her on the bed, caging her beneath him. She lifted her head from the pillow, meeting him halfway, matching his hungry kiss with one of her own. He was reminded of Halloween as the two of them gave in to the kisses, without bothering to rush to the next part.

They'd had the talk. Said all the words that needed to be said.

She was his. He was hers. They were in love.

Life simply didn't get any better than this.

Colm shifted lower, running his lips along the side of her neck down to her breasts. He took a nipple into his mouth, sucking, increasing the pressure until she gasped, her closed eyes flying open and meeting his.

"Making sure you're still awake," he teased.

"I'm not going to miss one second of this."

Colm smiled. He loved sparring with Kelli, but more than that, he loved the times like now, when she spoke sincerely, from the heart.

"I love you," he said, feeling the need to repeat those words to her a million times. Not because she needed to hear them but because he needed to say them.

Kelli ran her fingers over his cheek, stroking his beard. "Back atcha."

He played with her breasts, alternating between sucking, licking, and nipping until she was squirming beneath him.

"Colm," she breathed. "Please."

"Not yet," he murmured, moving even lower. He pressed on the insides of her knees, opening her more fully for him as he knelt between her outstretched legs. Her back arched when he placed his first open-mouthed kiss on her clit.

"Shit," she said. "So good!"

He flattened his tongue against the tiny nub, pushing more firmly, loving the way Kelli slowly came apart.

"Oh God. *Too* good," she gasped, her fists closed in his hair, pushing him away before pulling him closer again.

Colm increased the tempo of his tongue against her clit as he thrust inside her with two fingers, pumping faster with each return until Kelli stiffened for that one brief second, her mouth open in a silent scream, before her body trembled with her orgasm.

She cried out his name then, and he was sure he'd never heard a better sound in his life. There was nothing "peaceful" about the way Kelli yelled it, and he grinned to himself.

Dove, my ass, he thought with a grin as he felt the aftershocks of her climax, her inner muscles clenching against his fingers as he withdrew them.

Kelli was still struggling to catch her breath when he crawled back over her body to kiss her once more. Her face was flushed. She was hands down the most beautiful woman he'd ever seen.

It took everything he had not to thrust into her, to take her with all the passion and need she inspired, but tonight, this moment...

God, it was too important. Too special.

After several minutes of kissing, of sharing the same

sweet air, Colm forced his lips away from hers. His erection lay thick and hard against her stomach. He looked at her, waiting until Kelli's eyes slowly drifted open, and then even longer, until she was able to focus, her wits returning.

Colm brushed her cheek with his thumb, the other hand moving lower, gripping his cock until he'd placed the head of it at her body.

He didn't move, waiting.

Kelli was still. Too still.

Both of them were cognizant of the fact he wasn't wearing a condom, that what happened next would change both of their lives forever.

"Breathe," he whispered.

She gave him an adorable little grin, accompanied by one of those amused eyerolls she seemed to reserve just for him. "Need instructions?" she teased when he made no move to push inside.

He chuckled. "Are you ready to—"

"I swear to sweet Jesus," she interjected, "if you say 'transfer the funds' or some other ridiculous shit like that, I will cut your penis off right now."

Colm was holding himself above her on his elbows, his laughter shaking both of them as they lay chest to breasts on the bed. "I was going to say, are you ready to make our baby? I want a little girl, Kell. A carrot-top like you." Her eyes narrowed, hating when he referred to her hair as carrot-colored. "With my good looks, of course."

She gave him a sweet smile he instantly distrusted. "And I want a little boy who looks just like...Paddy."

"I think I can do that," he joked. They laughed briefly...

until he pressed inside just an inch. Then, once again, he was overwhelmed by all the emotions this beautiful, intelligent, headstrong, smart-ass of a woman inspired in him.

"I love you so much," he whispered as he thrust in, one long, slow glide. It felt *so* fucking good. He'd never taken a woman without a condom, and he knew he would never take Kelli with one again.

Once he was seated to the hilt, he paused for just a moment, trying to regain some semblance of control. This wouldn't take long, but he was bound and determined he wouldn't go down alone.

He placed his forehead against hers, both of them closing their eyes briefly. Then he shifted his hips and, for the first time in his life, he made love to a woman, to *the* woman...the friend, the enemy who'd claimed his heart, hook, line, and sinker.

They moved together, finding their rhythm naturally. Her body was made for his, and his for hers. Kelli's hands roamed over his shoulders, along the top of his arms, lightly scratching him, leaving her marks, as she whispered his name.

"Colm. God! I love you. Love you so much..."

Her words prodded him on. He needed more. Needed everything.

She *was* everything.

He took her harder, faster. Kelli planted her feet on the mattress by his knees, lifting her hips to meet him, silently demanding that he take even more.

"I...I'm," she chanted on a breath, letting him know she was there. She was ready.

"Me too," he said, reaching between them to stroke her

clit. He'd found that no-fail switch the very first night they were together. And now, like then, it drove her over the cliff, her back arching.

Her pussy clenched tightly against his cock, and Colm saw stars. Honest-to-God stars.

He came roughly, almost violently.

"Jesus. Kelli. Yes!"

It was agony and blinding bliss. He jerked, filling her, deafened by white noise and overwhelmed by the most intense pleasure he'd ever experienced.

By the time Colm returned to his senses, he was lying on his side, next to her, and Kelli was facing him, stroking his cheek, his beard with the back of her fingers.

She smiled. "You came inside me," she whispered, sounding happier than he'd ever heard her in his life.

Colm couldn't contain his own grin. "I did." Then he remembered something else. "Call Robbie. Tell him you don't need his help anymore."

"I already did. He was actually relieved since things with him and Brooke have gotten pretty hot and heavy."

"When did you call?" he asked.

"About three minutes after you left earlier."

"It took you three minutes?!" he said, acting appalled that it had taken her that long.

She raised the hand, touching his cheek in surrender. "I couldn't find my phone. It had fallen between the couch cushions."

"You're forgiven then." Colm shifted closer to her. They were already nearly nose to nose, but it wasn't enough for him. "We might have made a baby tonight, Kell."

"How cool would that be?"

"You're going to be an amazing mom."

"And you're going to be the world's greatest dad. Way better than mine. That's for sure."

Colm was reminded of earlier, her tone proving his gut feeling had been correct. Kelli had been hurt by her dad. "I'm never going to leave you, Kelli."

"Colm..." She started to shake her head, and he was worried that she was unable to believe his words as the truth. He understood why, but he still felt the need to reassure her.

"Look at me," he demanded.

Her lowered gaze raised to his.

"I'm *never* going to leave you."

He saw the hope buried deep in her eyes. "I know that," she admitted. "I know you."

"I know you're upset that he didn't call when he was in town."

She nodded slowly. "I can't understand why..." She shrugged one shoulder. "I always thought he stopped visiting, stopped calling because he didn't want to deal with my mom, but..."

Colm lifted her head with his finger under her chin. "I'm sorry."

She shook off the heaviness, smiling at him. If there was one thing about Kelli, the woman had a heck of a rebound. "It's okay. I sort of secretly stole your dad and made him mine years ago anyway."

"Not sure that was much of a secret," he joked. "You know, Dad would have kept having kids, would have kept going until he had a little girl—he said he always wanted a daughter—but Mom claimed chasing hellion twin boys broke her. You filled that void for him too."

He knew he'd found the words to make her feel better when her face lit up. "You think so?"

He nodded.

"I'd give you my mom too, but I think you're covered in that area," he added.

Kelli gave him a rueful grin. "Yeah. I think I have enough mother's love to last me until the end of time. I know I bitch about Barb a lot—"

"What?" Colm pretended to be shocked. "No."

"She doubled-down on the insane snowplow parenting after my dad left. I'm starting to understand why."

"Overcompensating?" he asked.

"Over-everything. But I know what my mom does is out of love for me. Sometimes I worry..." She didn't finish the thought, but he knew where her fears were leading.

"Genetics are not insurmountable, you know. You can be any kind of mother you want to be."

"I know. It's just...what if I go too far the other way? What if, in my attempt to not be crazy overbearing like my mom, I don't do enough for my kids?"

"That's what I'm here for. I'll keep you on the straight and narrow. And you'll do the same for me. We're in this together."

"Together," she repeated, as if she was trying out the sound of it. He and Kelli had both spent too many years as single units, independent people who answered only to themselves. It would probably take both of them some time to get a little less set in their ways. He couldn't wait to start.

In fact...

He gripped her waist and pulled her hips to his, loving the way she swung one leg over him. "Marry me."

She lifted her head from the pillow. "Was that a question or a demand?"

Colm moved his hand from her waist to her ass, gripping it tightly, holding her even closer. "Both," he murmured against her lips, kissing her. "I *need* you to marry me, Kelli. Need you to be my wife. I need it more than air."

She kissed him back. "You know, somehow you've managed to do all of this backwards. Lovers to friends, living together to dating, babies to marriage. You've made a mess of the whole thing, hotshot," she teased.

"Oh, *I* did, did I? Just me. Alone. Thanks for clarifying that." He tickled her until she cried uncle, then gave her another kiss. He was addicted to her lips. When he pulled away, he realized she hadn't responded. "You still haven't answered my question."

"I still haven't *heard* a question."

He playfully bit her shoulder. "You love to make me work for shit, don't you?"

"It's what makes life worth living."

"Will you marry me, Kelli? Have my babies, share my bed, and drive me crazy for the rest of my life?"

She pretended to consider, acting as if it was a really hard decision.

"Bear in mind, I own a lot of neckties, and I would have no trouble tying you to this bed and spanking your ass until you agree."

"Wow. I was going to say yes, but I'm suddenly thinking I might need more convincing."

He narrowed his eyes. "Say yes and I'll *still* tie you up and spank your ass."

"Yes."

"Marry me soon."

She rolled her eyes heavenward. "God, you're a demanding ass."

"*Soon*, Kelli," he stressed. "Very soon."

"Fine. Soon."

EPILOGUE

"Hey, Pop Pop," Colm said, peeking his head in through his grandfather's open bedroom door. He'd moved in with Aunt Riley and Uncle Aaron when they built an addition onto the back of their house, creating a little suite for him. Now he spent most of his time there, with Bubbles as his daytime companion, the two of them playing rummy and watching way too much reality TV, though neither of them would ever confess to that. In the evenings, he'd watch sports either here with Aaron or at the pub, surrounded by family and the regular patrons.

Pop Pop glanced up from the romance novel he was reading, tucking it under the pillow with a guilty grin. The entire family was aware of his penchant for steamy romance novels, even though Pop Pop insisted he was reading mysteries and thrillers.

"Well, this is a nice surprise. What brings you here, lad?" Pop Pop stood up and gestured to the small sitting area in his room. Colm took one chair, his grandfather the other.

"Kelli had her sonogram today. I wanted to come by and tell you..." Colm paused, grinning, still struggling to believe the news himself. "Twins. She's having *twins*."

Pop Pop's eyes lit up and he clapped his hands together. "Bless my soul. Twins! That's wonderful news."

"Yeah. Kelli's over the moon. I've never seen her so happy."

"And you?"

Colm's smile grew wider. "Dream come true."

"It is indeed. Oh," Pop Pop stood up again, "I almost forgot. I wanted to show you something."

Colm rose and followed his grandfather to the special wall. One entire wall of his bedroom was covered with photographs of the family, each member represented.

The photographs changed from time to time, based only on Pop Pop's whims, rather than to mark celebrations or special occasions. Unlike most people, he didn't frame posed senior portraits or wedding photos. All of Pop Pop's pictures were candids; brief moments in time that, according to Pop Pop, captured the essence of the person photographed.

Pop Pop raised his finger and pointed to Colm's frame. For the past several years, it had been a picture of Colm sitting at the pub, a pint in front of him as he talked to Padraig one day after work. He'd been wearing a suit, his tie loosened, and he was kicked back, relaxed, smiling. He'd asked Pop Pop at the time why he'd chosen it. After all, it was a simple photo that seemed to show very little. Just him at the bar.

Pop Pop insisted it was the perfect photograph. That he

saw an intelligent, family-oriented man who was comfortable in his own skin, self-assured, successful, and on the brink of greatness.

Colm hadn't known how to respond at the time, but when he'd looked at the picture again, he'd seen it through his grandfather's loving eyes, and it suddenly hadn't felt so simple after all.

This time, the picture was different.

"Where did you get that?" Colm asked, somewhat surprised to see that Pop Pop hadn't updated his photo with a current picture of him and Kelli. There would have been plenty to choose from. He could have used the one of the two of them at Christmas, announcing their engagement. Or one of the small wedding ceremony they'd held at the pub in January. Or even one of the two of them revealing that Kelli was pregnant at a family dinner on Valentine's Day.

Instead, Pop Pop had somehow found an old photograph of him and Kelli, sitting in his parents' backyard at a summer picnic. He remembered the day well because they'd just graduated from high school the week before, and they were both excited and ready to head off to college.

Kelli was laughing and talking to him—with her hands flying, of course, one of which held a hot dog. Colm was sitting next to her. She had ketchup on her mouth, and he'd reached over to wipe it off with his finger.

For nearly fifteen years, the picture had been relegated to a slot in one of his mom's countless photo albums, forgotten.

Colm didn't have to ask why Pop Pop had chosen it. The answer was written right there in Colm's eighteen-year-old eyes. His younger self was grinning like a fool...and looking at Kelli as if she hung the moon.

He couldn't ever recall consciously thinking of her that way, but had he?

God knew he looked at her like that now. Every freaking second of the day.

She'd become his world, and his only regret in life was that the stupid teenager in this photo hadn't leaned forward and wiped that ketchup away with his tongue...followed by a kiss.

"So many wasted years," he murmured.

"Oh no, son. That's not what I see at all. I see two head-strong, stubborn, independent people who had a lot of life to live before they could see and truly appreciate what they'd found. This moment...it was just the beginning of your story. An epic tale."

"Complete with blackouts, karaoke, wine, and babies."

Pop Pop laughed. "As well as laughter, friendship and love. The best kind of story. Because it has a happy ending."

"I love the picture." They both looked at it for a moment longer before returning to their chairs.

"Twins," Pop Pop said quietly. Like Colm, it seemed as if the only way for Pop Pop to truly believe it was to say the word over and over a few thousand times. It still hadn't sunk in for Colm either. It was just too good to be true.

"So," Pop Pop said. "It sounds like your father's prayers for you when you were a teenager have come true."

Colm tilted his head, curious. "Prayers?"

"He always said he hoped you had children just like you," Pop Pop said with a wink.

Colm laughed. "I think you and I both know that wasn't a prayer, Pop Pop. It was a curse."

Pop Pop reached out and patted Colm's hand. "And you and I both know...it's not."

"You're right. It's not. But telling you about the babies isn't the reason I came here. At least, not the *only* reason. You and I have some work to do."

"We do?"

"Yeah. Names. If these babies are boys, I want names that mean something tough. None of these stone or dove names. Something rugged. Like a gladiator. Or maybe even a god."

Colm chuckled to himself as a name popped into his mind.

Kelli would kill him.

"What's Thor mean?"

DON'T MISS out on Darcy's story, Wild Embrace, coming Oct. 2020. You can preorder it now!

HAVE you read the entire Wilder Irish series? All the books are standalone, so they can be read in any order. Be sure to check out all of them!

Wild Passion - FREE

Wild Desire

Wild Devotion

Wild at Heart

Wild Temptation

Wild Kisses

Wild Fire
Wild Spirit
Wild Side
Wild Night

FANS OF WILD Irish AND Facebook! There's a group for you. Come join the Wild Irish Facebook group for sneak peaks, cover reveals, contests and more! Join now.

BE sure to join my newsletter for a FREE Wilder Irish short story.

WILD EMBRACE

Love is full of bad clichés.

Falling for your boss.

The widowed dad and the nanny.

How did Darcy manage to find both of them in Ryder Hagan?

His broken heart and wounded pride means he only sees her as an employee in his company and part-time caregiver for his sons.

Until another cliché surprises them both:

The old broken elevator trap.

And the wild attraction he's kept buried begins to break out.

Can his perfectly ordered life survive discovering love again?

Preorder Wild Embrace.

ABOUT THE AUTHOR

Virginia native Mari Carr is a New York Times and USA TODAY bestseller of contemporary erotic romance novels. With over one million copies of her books sold, Mari was the winner of the Romance Writers of America's Passionate Plume award for her novella, Erotic Research. She has over a hundred published works, including her popular Wild Irish and Compass books, along with the Trinity Masters/Masters Admiralty series she writes with Lila Dubois.

Find Mari Carr on the web at
www.maricarr.com
mari@maricarr.com

Made in the USA
Monee, IL
16 June 2020

33800340R00132